THE PROSPECTED FAMILY

VOLUMES FROM THE VOID

BOOK I

MIKE EKSTROM

BLACK BRICK BOOKS, LLC

Black Brick Books, LLC
author@blackbrickbooks.com
volumesfromthevoid.com

Paperback ISBN: 979-8-9905694-1-6
Hardcover ISBN: 979-8-9905694-0-9
Ebook ISBN: 979-8-9905694-2-3

Cover and interior design by Jess LaGreca, Mayfly book design
Edited by Suzanne Coner

Library of Congress Catalog Number: 2024908164

First Printing: 2024

CONTENTS

For Mom and Dad,
Chris, my wonderfully supportive partner,
and my sister, Megan.

This one's for you.

CHAPTER 1

THE FIFTH ITERATION

"We should make another. Don't you think?" the words came from an ethereal whisper—a woman's voice. The blackness of absolution sung with the harmonious hum of her question.

"Why don't we make a pair of twins—one to reflect the other," came a deep, impatient growl; the man's throat boomed in response, sending a stir through the Darkness.

Immediately, the feminine response almost mockingly cooed, "You mean a man *and* a woman?"

"It would keep the Balance. What's the worst that could happen this time?" he grumbled lowly and sighed, annoyed but not upset.

Suddenly, the blackness turned upside down and was washed away in a blinding flood of white light, as the two celestial entities together exhaled their energies—one of Darkness and one of Life. The haze of chaos and entropy that weaved together to create the fabric of reality shifted as creation, destiny, and Time unraveled and wound together again. Winds of Life swirled in the remaining bodies of Darkness, and six orbs of energy were conceived in the nothingness of Time, each of them a different color. Red, orange, green, blue, violet, and magenta.

These two beings materialized in the nothingness, like giants appearing in the sky, in a place known only as the Void of Impossible Things—an in-between world created out of accident from which Time originated. The man stood enormously tall and upright, with a greying black beard and jet-black hair and eyes. His cheeks sagged with wisdom and age like anchors in deep waters. His tanned skin was rough and covered with a heavy set of leather robes that wrapped loosely around his body, which stood broadly like a heavy tree. The woman, his opposite, stood as tall, but a little shorter, with a hunch in her shoulders as if locked in pensive concentration. Her hair was smooth and pure white. It cascaded down her back, like a silken waterfall. Her pale skin complimented her piercing electric blue eyes. She wore a delicate, tulip-yellow dress, that was not elaborate or exquisite in any way. Her thin frame clung to any sign of youthfulness it could. The man and the woman stood in the center of these six spheres; each round ball hummed and danced with pent-up energy. As the man brought his hands up to meet the woman's they locked eyes and clasped each other's fingers. Once their skin touched, color radiated from their fingertips, and fed each of the six bodies a unique hue.

"The Fifth Iteration," the soft, female voice whispered. Through her words was a hint of exasperation, a longing for rest, but otherwise, her words still sang with an innocent serenity.

"Good riddance! It should be our last!" The man's voice suddenly boomed with dominance. Impatience faded, he sounded upset. "Our children should be masterpieces this time, Mother. A Family, fit to rule with assertion. Each facet of our children has been painstakingly carved with Time, Darkness, and Life."

"Patience, Father," The female's decree reassured him. "Our children still need their gifts, *our gifts*. Otherwise they'll be of no use to us. Masterpieces take effort, and we've spent enough energy toiling over their genesis. This Iteration, I expect, will be our perfection. They are prospected to do great things—to take on the helm of the Universe. The Prospected Family."

The six orbs began to change shapes as they grew into torsos which bore arms and legs and a head sprouted on top. The colors and lights sunk into the chest cavities of each shaping body as their hue became more and more pronounced. The first to fully take shape was a tall, slender woman. Her eyes burned red like furious embers, and her skin was pale and soft—a stark difference from her bushy, blackened-auburn hair. She wafted in a scarlet cloud as she lazily watched the next sibling take shape, as Father announced boldly, "Helena, the Weakest. The keeper of the After-Life. The overseer of the dead, born to create from that which is already created." Then he added more wistfully, "My dearest child." She wore a short, thick leather cloak that conformed to her body well.

Another woman, this one bathed in a blue light, stretched her limbs out. Her body was wrapped in silk linens that clung to her figure like a toga. She was shorter than her reddened sister and had the same pale skin, but had Mother's waist-length, pearl-white hair, and electric blue eyes. She floated in a sea of cyan energy that billowed out from her pores.

"Madrina," Mother murmured. "My daughter, my image, my legacy." Father scoffed in her direction and flung his arm forward eagerly as the next of their children emerged from the swirling blur of light.

Quickly after, a burst of acid-green light gave birth to a proud-looking, tall man, with greasy-black hair and grey skin that seemed to smoke and smolder. His eyes were deep emerald pools that pierced with a stern stare. He was filled with youth, brimming with it. He wore ragged, worn shorts and a narrow vest that revealed his muscled chest. He sat in a pool of slick, green oil, waiting.

"The Hunter," Mother began. When she kept her sentiments to herself, Father spoke up.

"The one whose touch can burn. Born to bring death to Life, and to keep order and balance among all existence," he said proudly of his son, the child with no name.

Next, another man was created unceremoniously in a blast of orange light. He seemed to mimic Mother's pale, hunched appearance, but had Father's neat, black hair. He looked modest, his rich, amber-colored eyes seemed to convey a sadness that was lost under deep folds of thought. Tailored to his body was an expertly woven white shirt and shorter shorts than his brother wore—neater too.

"Davias, the Thinker; he who shall be by my side in the Pre-Life as we see to the rebirth of souls into Life," Mother's voice sang sweetly again, as if his birth brought her new meaning. Surrounding him was a halo of orange light, like a sunrise came from within his body.

All eyes gazed at the last two spheres, which pulsed and intensified as they illuminated and revealed a pair of figures situated in such a way they were staring at each other with identical pairs of gentle, violet-colored eyes. One of them was male and the other was female, and they looked exactly like each other; short with ratty grey hair and a tanned complexion. Both of them held a long, wooden oar like the ones used to steer a large boat, and as they slowly drifted apart, their two colors became more distinct. His was a deep purple, and hers turned out to be a bright shade of magenta. They both wore tattered and frayed clothing that hung in ribbons off of their skinny bodies. Surrounding both of them were crystalline bubbles—transparent but stained like glass with their respective hues.

"The Watchers—Elias and Eliza. Our twins of the River Styx, born to watch over the dead, the living, and those traveling in between," Mother explained to no one in particular. As if in response, the surrounding whiteness began to rumble and shake with ferocity as one by one, each of the six siblings disappeared in a bolt of their own color, leaving Mother and Father staring alone and directly at each other. Knowingly, they clapped their hands, and all of the white began to bleed into a mixture as Mother and Father both disappeared from the Void of Impossible Things.

Two floating bodies of land emerged through the bleeding colors, both as magnificent as the other. The After-Life; an area dusty and grungy in appearance, covered in storms with a bruised, maroon and brown canopy for a sky. Its terrain was infinite and rocky, spotted with black slates of obsidian that jutted out at every which angle and canopied by a single, ever-expanding gray cloud. The other landmass, the Pre-Life, was a much smaller monument to beauty: An island with an exquisite open skyline, a pristine landscape adorned with golden meadows and beautiful flora, and a rippling river that carved gently through the landscape. The river, known as the River Styx, was the passageway between Realms—the living and the celestial. The Void of Impossible Things ran like a thin veil between these two land masses—like a transparent, shimmering wall that wrapped around this entire realm.

Davias had joined his siblings—Madrina, Elias, and his twin Eliza—waiting for Mother in the Pre-Life near the banks of the River Styx. A long, wooden craft appeared on the water's edge and bobbed gently on the surface.

. . .

Helena dug her heel impatiently into the barren, red dirt of the After-Life's dry landscape. As her impatience grew, she crossed her arms across her chest and began to pace in the dust. Her bushy, dark hair bobbed with every move. Even more annoying to her than Father's inexplicable absence was the immense volume of dismally-colored spheres that seemed to occupy every other meter in the After-Life, some rolling along the ground while some floated miserably in the air. A number of these spheres smoldered and left a trail of ash in their wake, and others didn't move at all. Helena's short, pointed nose tilted high in the air as she scoffed silently and rolled her red eyes. She uncrossed her arms to tuck her hair behind one of her ears indignantly.

Just then, Father's voice boomed behind her, causing her to jump out of fright. "Helena! My favorite daughter. Welcome to your home—the After-Life. Our home, together." He extended his arms outward to both of his sides and spun in a small circle on the spot as if in celebration, but Helena was not impressed. She glanced around at the surrounding scenery; it was barren, vast, and covered in thick black rocks and rolling spheres as far as she could see.

Helena turned around and craned her face upwards to look at Father. At this angle, her bony cheeks and sunken eyes cast deep shadows across her face, making her irises glow through the shade. "What am I doing here? I don't want to be surrounded by these . . . things."

"If it would help, I know a better place we can go, closer to the edge. There's fewer souls there but, Helena, you would be wise to get used to them." Father began walking, taking large strides with his enormous legs that forced his daughter to hurry along in his wake, taking extra care to delicately avoid a soul that meandered into their path.

"Why is that, Father?" her voice tried to disguise her disgust, but Father saw through this façade with ease.

He closed his eyes and smiled solemnly and heavily. "The After-Life is a sanctuary for the souls that have run the course of their mortality. There are billions and billions of them in our wide expanse—a small handful of them are as ancient as Time and are almost as old as myself. The souls will arrive here after their course on Life, hence the name—but Life can change certain fundamental characteristics. So, think of this place as a facility to sort out the wicked souls from the innocent. Rehabilitation for the already dead and damned."

She breathily asked him, "What do we do with the wicked souls? The evil ones? Twisted beyond mercy."

"We keep them imprisoned—Life is a privilege for only a few billion at a time in order to maintain the Balance, and while imprisoned, we aim to leverage reformation and reconciliation of even the most twisted beings until they are ready for Life again."

"And the innocent ones?" Helena continued to take monstrous-sized strides as quickly as she could to try and keep up with Father's pace. At times, the speeds she was taking were at a full run.

"Mother and Davias are waiting for them in the Pre-Life, so they can be reincarnated—given back to Life again. The cycle must continue; there exists a balance between Life and our Realm, and it is a thinly divided scale. Mother and I have seen past Iterations fail because the Balance was ill-tended."

"So what's stopping me from leaving this place, then? Am I going to be obliterated if I jump off the edge?"

"Helena, my dear daughter, I know you are reluctant to accept your responsibilities now, but I have ambitious plans for you, some that I hope will assuage your opinions of your duties. But you cannot willingly leave this place, there are certain rules about the comings and goings in our Realm—the Watchers have the sole privilege of travelling to and from. As for what lies over the edge, that would be the Void. Falling in there would most certainly mean getting trapped or obliterated. I'm not too certain what the real outcome would be, but I imagine it would not be pleasant for you. Now, we're nearly there. Come, let me first show you how it is we send our souls back to the Pre-Life for their reincarnation."

Helena refused and stopped abruptly in her tracks, forcing Father to turn around while he was already several paces ahead.

"Who do you think you are, Father? What do you think you know about me? Can I just be myself, or must I submit to the image of me that you already have in your head?" She shouted. He stopped in midstride and pivoted towards her, leaning down lower in the process of doing so.

Father peered down at her while he raised an eyebrow in confusion. "Who said anything about disallowing your individuality? As a matter of fact, Helena, I intend to hone your individuality, to harness it in order to accomplish great things. What do I know of you? I know plenty. I am going to weaponize you, my daughter. They call you 'the Weakest,' but do you even know what you're capable of, or will I need to show you the true meaning of your existence?"

She crossed her arms and doubled down on her assertion. "Show me, Father."

"No. At least not yet. You've much to learn, and I think it best if we start with the most basic. This way," Father proceeded back in the direction they were headed. Helena was too winded from trying to keep pace to say anything when they arrived. A bare plateau made up of a series of interlocking black slates stretched out far, and, as promised, the number of nearby souls had diminished to a small handful gathered around the middle of the stones. Father had stopped walking. He was lumbering high above the ring of depressed-looking spheres, and he watched as Helena hurried to catch up, tentatively approaching the souls with carefully executed movements.

"What is this place?" she asked absent-mindedly with a mixture of curiosity and awe. Then added, "Why do I feel like I've been here before?"

"Because you have been here before. Mother and I—there had to be some damage control," Father stammered awkwardly, unable to find the words he was looking for. He maintained his eye contact, which told Helena the vastness of what he was telling her. "What you need to know is we are going to do things differently—everyone, so that we can maintain the Balance and maintain control of the After-Life. That is our burden to bear." With those words, Father knelt down, which brought him eye level with Helena, and he took one of her hands in his palms and squeezed, bringing a blackness to her fingertips.

"This is just a touch of my Essence. Darkness—it is an energy along with Life that resides within you—within all living things, mortal or otherwise. Darkness is the first element in the cycle back to Life. With just a small touch, we give a modicum of our energy unto the helpless; we impregnate the perfect with fallacies, and with that we give them purpose. We birth their destinies. But, like you and your siblings, they will lose their memories in the transition, too."

She leered at Father angrily, as if she had recollection of this. "You took my memories from me," she spouted. "Are you trying to hide something?"

Father responded to her anger with an aggression of his own. Still holding her hand, he squeezed tightly, causing bones to pop. "Your brothers' memories were taken, too, so don't feel like you've been singled out! There were many transgressions from you kids. Mother and I made the difficult decision to isolate as many of you as possible in this Iteration, and now that is everyone's consequence to bear whether you remember or not. The decision was difficult because it isolates all of us, and it will make our work longer. Now, let's get on with it!" He took her broken hand, and one by one forcibly made contact with each of the surrounding souls, whose dismal colors changed spontaneously with contact. One changed into a yellow orb, two changed into different shades of green. There was a blue, a white, and a bright red as well that Helena was immediately fond of as her face lit with amusement upon seeing a familiar hue.

One by one, the souls lifted into the air and darted forward past the edge of the After-Life, heading straight for the shimmering wall that separated the Pre-Life from its counterpart. They pierced through the Void of Impossible Things with ease, and disappeared from view as they continued fluttering onwards. The two of them watched wordlessly with differing levels of investment. Father was still knelt down beside Helena. He broke the silence with his deep growl.

"That, daughter, is all you have to do. When I tell you to, you will come to this exact spot, and send the souls waiting for you here onward to the Pre-Life. You do this with grace, and I will reward you just as graciously. Refuse, and your rewards will be as absent as your efforts. Do I make myself clear?" His last sentence was enunciated as he emphasized his seriousness. He arched an eyebrow as he awaited his daughter's hesitant response.

"Yes, Father," Helena submitted. "But . . . I do have one question."

Father looked at Helena with an eyebrow creeping higher in suspicion. "You may ask."

"You said 'this Iteration.' How many others have there been?" she recalled.

"Four, this is the Fifth Iteration—the last Mother and I will ever do."

Helena thought again for a brief moment before asking another question. "Why is it going to be the last?"

For once, Father's defenses fell, and rather than being suspicious or angry with his daughter, he was bemused. "*I never said it was going to be the last.* I said it was going to be my last because, my dear, I am bored with creating and tired of fighting. I am tired of the lies and tired of creating and destroying and starting over again. I watch Time trickle by like a creek in the desert—always taunting, but never satisfying me. Unlike you children who were born in the Void of Impossible Things, I can't ever experience the passage of Time, Helena. I am older than existence itself, and it is about time for me to retire and pass my responsibilities along. To you.”

“What would I be responsible for—besides the After-Life and these . . . souls?” again, a hint of disgust peppered most of her speech.

Father peered out over the edge towards the Pre-Life once more and grumbled, “Your siblings. Gather the ones you can; I may be tired of fighting, but that doesn’t mean I can’t lead the charge.”

“And how am I supposed to do that if I am confined to this . . . place?” her attitude in her tone was aggressive. Father decided to answer her attitude with some of his own. He paid her a mere glancing look and then proceeded in the direction the two of them had come from. As he retreated, he raised his voice in authoritative nonchalance.

“I really don’t care, nor do I care how long it takes. We have Time on our side, so let’s gather the forces and get to work. I want you to use your abilities to build something for me. Something big.”

CHAPTER 2

THE PRE-LIFE

In the center of a serene, majestic meadow, speckled with patches of golden, shimmering grass and flora so flawless they sparkled like glass, stood a magnificent-looking tree—easily over one hundred feet tall with an obtuse, fat trunk and several thousand thick, twisted branches. The leaves glittered with every possible color and the light reflected off of the surface like a diamond and each refraction looked like a spark thrown from a fire. Madrina stood patiently waiting underneath the low-hanging branches of the tree that provided the most shade. Around her, a couple dozen very colorful souls danced around playfully and merrily, free from any worry.

"Hey, Davias," she said as her younger brother strode past, completely unaware of her presence. Hearing his name pulled him out of his deep concentration, and his head whipped around to see his silk-shrouded, silver-haired sister waving gently in his direction.

"What are you doing here, Ma—Ma—" he struggled with her name. It was there. He knew it, but it was new to him, somehow. He abandoned whatever route he was taking and walked over to meet her. Her slender, frail-looking figure was outlined and lit up by the light show around her.

"Ma—dree—na," she said a little slowly. "It's okay. I know you, too, but I can't remember much about anything. It's quite beautiful here. I like it."

"What are you doing here, anyway?" he asked her again. Whether he meant to sound rude or not didn't seem to matter to him. It didn't seem to matter to his sister, either, as she responded pleasantly.

"I'm catching a ride with the twins, but first, I understand Mother has some words for me."

Davias' ears perked at Mother's mention. "I was waiting for her, too. I'm not sure what I'm supposed to do here. Or what he's supposed to be doing here, either." Davias motioned behind Madrina as he approached her in the shade and dazzling lights. His sister craned her head around to watch the Hunter approaching in the distance; a black aura emanated from his body like a faint, fuzzy outline.

"Hello, darlings," he sneered obnoxiously as he approached.

"What in Father's name are you doing here?" Madrina called back to him.

His grey skin appeared to bubble and ripple down his arms. He ran the fingers of one of his hands through his hair and tossed it to the side a little before answering. "The same thing you are— I can't leave this place on my own, as much as I wish I could. So I need to catch a ride out of this forsaken cage."

"Why don't you like this place? It's serene," Davias defended the meadow and all of its beauty and innocence. Madrina looked as if she were equally offended.

"Brother, serenity is for the weak. My gifts don't belong in our Realm. I belong out there, in Life. Hunting people, killing things. I am useless here. I tell you, we've barely even been here, and I already feel confined. I need to wreak havoc and cause calamity. Blood will be spilled the moment I can get my hands on a mortal."

"Well you're certainly eager, aren't you? Look, here come the twins," she remarked with a disgusted tone as Madrina pointed to the River Styx nearby, whose bend came close to the tree they resided under. A long, wooden-paneled gondola emerged around the curve through a thin fog. The twins stood proudly on top of the boat, dipping their oars in the water and propelling themselves across the surface. The two of them stood back-to-back, mirroring each other's movements in synchronized fashion.

"Finally. Now I can get out of here," the Hunter pouted as he kicked a divot into the pristine landscape in an effort to send a golden stone flying.

Davias looked at him with the most quizzical look. "I just don't understand your eagerness to leave, Hunter."

He scowled towards the river's edge, disgruntled by his sibling's efforts to try and understand him. "Perhaps you never will. Perhaps you shouldn't, Thinker, but no matter," he moved closer to the bank without looking backwards. His breath shook his body with anticipation. "I have little to do with you, anyways, so why waste your time on me?"

As the boat drew nearer, Mother seemed to step out of the veil of mist that blanketed the water. Her majestic figure glided gently over the ground—though she stood at a gigantic height of nine feet, her silver-haired head hardly appeared to sway. Her blue eyes beamed in the heavenly light, and she walked at pace on the river bank with the twins' on their gondola. The three of them came to a head at the end of the bend in the River Styx. Madrina, Davias, and the Hunter all looked onward at the arrival of their family.

"Mother!" Davias and Madrina greeted almost in unison. The boat pulled ashore, and the two siblings disembarked simultaneously—still mimicking the other's movements as they both hopped off of opposite ends with their long wooden oars in hand.

Mother greeted them all with a harmonious hum and a tranquil bow of her head. "Hello, you five. Elias, if you wouldn't mind taking the Hunter to the ferry, I have some business to discuss with your sisters and Davias here."

Eli nodded obediently and silently returned to the craft while the Hunter raised his voice in protest. "I'm not waiting here any longer than I absolutely have to! Keep it short, Mother, I have business to attend to as well!"

"Hunter, my child, I know the kind of business you dabble in—the importance of our work far outweighs your impatience to hunt. Go, wait on the boat with your brother. You'll soon be on your way." Mother watched and waited until her two boys were safely out of earshot before she turned to the trio of siblings waiting dutifully at her feet. Mother turned her attention towards the horizon as six streamers of color ripped through the air as individual spheres of light hurled towards them and came to an abrupt, hovering halt just a few feet off of the ground. They spun calmly in the middle of everyone as Mother began speaking in a hushed tone. "My apologies for being so short with you, but Hunter is in a rush, and so are we. Each of you has a job to do. Each of your jobs involves these—these are Human souls. Davias, you and I will spend some time with each of them, giving them personality, erasing past memories, carefully sending them to where they need to go. Life is a vast place, and each soul plays a part in the Balance. Eliza, once the souls are ready, you and Eli are poised to travel through the Void by way of the River Styx to take them back to Life, and while you are there, the Hunter will bring you souls to transport back to the After-Life on your next trip. And when you two return, Davias and I will have more to send back—a never-ending cycle of Life, After-Life, and Pre-Life."

"Mother?" Madrina interrupted rather timidly. Mother arced an eyebrow—her way of wordlessly expressing her expectation for more context. "You said we all had a job? You haven't told me what role I play, yet."

From her palm, Mother procured a pure, flawless-looking white gem—long and intricately faceted. She offered it to Madrina, as if this was the answer to her question. In response, her daughter took it in both hands without question or complaint, and in moments, the crystal began to dissolve. "Your job, Madrina, should become rather apparent to you the moment you take this. What I need you to do is escort this blue soul to Life and guard him. When you can, I'll need you to build something for me; it'll require quite a bit of work. I'm giving you some of my energy—my Life—so we can communicate across the Void. Before you pass the Void completely, you need to bless that soul." There was an authoritative urgency in her commands, and a hushed silence fell over her audience following her words. "Eliza?" She asked with the same sternness.

"Yes, Mother?" the youngest daughter replied.

"You are a Watcher. I need you to keep an eye on the Hunter's comings and goings, and—as much as it pains me to ask this of you—don't turn a blind eye towards Eli's intentions, either. Keep a low profile among them, but if either of them begins to act . . . erratically, I want you to tell me, Madrina, or Davias, whoever you can right away." Eliza nodded with confidence and threw Mother a strong salute. "Now hurry along to the boat." Mother paused, pursing her lips, then continued. "And Eliza . . . don't lose that oar." The youngest daughter skipped away without another sound, carrying the large wooden oar awkwardly as she went.

A swift breeze cascaded through the branches of the tree above them, casting an audible ripple through the leaves that grabbed Mother's attention. "The two of you need to know something else before we part ways. It will be some time before the three of us are together again. There are certain events that are already in motion that are going to conceive other events. The history and mechanics behind everything are beyond convoluted and predate you two by several millennia. There is a schism in this Family that I hope you and your siblings fall on the right side of. If you listen to me, we can preserve the Balance and the integral beauty of the Fifth Iteration. Without the Balance, we will see everything get laid to waste. There is a reason I will be asking Eliza for frequent updates on your brothers." Mother stared at both of her children in an attempt to get her point across.

Heeding her words as a very steep warning, Madrina and Davias reciprocated her eye contact and waited for her to say more. After a moment of silence, Mother closed her eyes and took a deep, relaxing breath. "Madrina, you should join your siblings on the boat and get going—we don't want to keep Hunter waiting, and we have to get busy. Remember what you need to do." Madrina took off towards the boat after hesitating for another moment. As she retreated, the half dozen souls responded by following her in a single file line aboard the gondola, which began moving autonomously the moment the last passenger was in place.

Taken aback by his sudden privacy with Mother, Davias found himself basking in the tranquility and picturesque scenery. He closed his eyes, and all he could hear was the rippling of the River Styx interrupted by the occasional breeze through the branches. He could smell the purity of the water wafting through the air— the air itself felt cool, with a slight mist to its touch, which embraced his body like a cool bath. His mouth filled with the botanical tastes of the meadow and the river's mist with each deep breath he took.

"What do you think of the Pre-Life?" he heard her voice softly inquire from somewhere behind him. He took his time in answering, trying to find the appropriate words to express his experience in that particular moment.

"Being here is like balancing on the edge in between satisfaction and peace. I have a very profound feeling that I have been here before, in quite the similar fashion, but I'm also thinking that isn't possible. Which is it?"

Mother nodded silently and reached her arm behind her back and motioned at the grand tree standing behind her. "This is the Tree of Knowledge, Davias. Within its roots are the most important and best-kept histories and secrets, told through Time, thought lost through death but preserved here in the Pre-Life. The grandest collection that ever existed."

"I thought the Pre-Life was for returning souls back to Life? Continuing the cycle for the innocent and maintaining the Balance all the while. Not some tales and stories."

Mother clicked her tongue condescendingly while casting an approving look over her son. "You remembered some things from before—overall, that'll make this easier. You're not wrong, Davias, but where the After-Life is used to store souls, the Pre-Life is where we store their legacies. We have to keep them separated, or else the souls will remember their previous lives. Do you remember the Library?" Davias shook his head in the negative. "Never mind about that right now, then, you'll see it when you're ready. Do you remember your duties?" This time he nodded.

"I wouldn't say I remember anything, Mother. It's more as if I understand deeply, as if I had been told this all before. That being said, I understand what I am supposed to do: process the souls upon their arrival and send them off to the After-Life where I assume Helena and Father will do the opposite, and when they do, I am to receive those souls, and after processing them, send them to Eliza and Elias where they are then reincarnated back into Life."

"Like clockwork. I am glad you retained all of that. Now, can you tell me what went wrong before?"

Davias thought long and hard in silence. He carefully wrapped one hand's fingers around his chin as he pressed his memory into the foggiest crevices that he could. "I don't know, but I feel like there's something missing." He removed his hand and kept fidgeting.

Mother pulled him into a reassuring embrace. "There are many things missing—there are many things to be done. Will you help me in seeing to our success?"

"Yes," he said simply with a sweet and innocent smile stretched across his mouth as he pulled back from her. Mother responded with a smile of her own and she slid one of her large, elegant hands down his back and gently pushed him forward towards the water's still surface. The two of them peered over the edge and stared at the reflections of their own faces with the beauty of the Pre-Life emanating from around them and the branches from the Tree of Knowledge that overlooked them.

"I don't know what you remember—or what was forgotten during the last Iteration, so I'll need to go over a few details with you before we get to work. Do you remember where Father and I come from? Our origin?" Davias shook his head, and Mother cast her palm over the surface of the river, and the water became an illustrious canvas that morphed and changed with Mother's every word. She moved behind her son and grabbed hold of both of his shoulders so she could carefully show him the illustrations on the water's surface. She whispered gently in his ear as she narrated the passing story:

"In the First Iteration, there was nothing, and nothing was all there was. Father and I lived by ourselves in the celestial world, and as it was, it was really just the two of us. Father—the Darkness—and myself—the Life. Two counterweights on the same balance, and in the beginning, the two of us lived together in isolated harmony. Father's embodiment afforded him magnitude and dominance in such a way that my finite body could only move so little—I was embodied in a large round shell. A planet now called Earth, my body once glowed with the majesty of the energy that pulsed through me. Life. What a bountiful resource!

And Father knew it, and he was envious of me. So much, to the point that he began to taunt me, teasing me and my slow body. Until I had an idea to turn the tricks back on him. I used my energy—Life—to create more spheres that looked like me. At first, it was a few hundred, just enough to confuse the Darkness. But the more and more that strategy worked, the more and more I employed it, creating billions and trillions of different planets along the way.

"That proved to be my undoing, however. Our undoing, rather. The problem with me creating too much wasn't that I did or didn't do anything wrong; it was that Father didn't do his part in providing balance. Him not creating or destroying anything led to a schism in the celestial Universe—a crack in the crust that holds all of reality in the same construct. I created the Void of Impossible Things, while at the same time, I ushered Father and myself into the Second Iteration with haste."

While watching the images move like oil on the water's surface, Davias couldn't help but interrupt the tale. "So the Iterations weren't always intentional?"

"No, they weren't. You'll see that more often than not, we had no idea what we were doing—our existence was reactionary; we were never proactive."

He turned to face Mother with childlike enthusiasm. "Is that what I am here for? To be proactive and to provide you with your Balance?"

"As it were, both yes and no. Your siblings and yourself are the help in the chaos Father and I created. You don't provide the Balance to the Family—the Family must all work in unison to *maintain* the Balance. We didn't immediately realize that reality had changed, until the two of us observed something new: Time. Time had emerged from the crack created in the world, and we watched it slowly decay and change all that was around us without ever affecting us. The planets that I had created had begun to die, and my haste had only stirred Father's anger—and so he pressed Darkness even further into the edges of the Universe. His recklessness and the need for him to try to destroy what I created forced me to create more bodies, but I was emboldened by my own lessons learned. I crafted stars to make light. Light scared away the Darkness, and after a while, the two of us began to find our own balance, but that, once again, came at another great price. Father's recklessness to spread Darkness as thin as possible and my repeated mistake to create haphazardly caused the rift in the Universe to widen so violently and suddenly that it split reality in two. Our Realm, and the Realm below us. That split was also so violent that it ripped the remaining energies out of our bodies, and our corpses remained where they were— my body, Life, is the only planet of its kind. The only one that can sustain souls as an appropriate host, and it orbits a modest star, close enough to keep Father's Darkness from swallowing it. Close enough to provide an equal balance to the Humans. Everywhere that Father had once managed to spread Darkness, there it will forever be.

"We were exiled to the new Realm—and what we found was just as confusing as it was astounding. Our destination was our home as it is now—the Pre-Life and the After-Life, separated by the source of the rift, a lake of silver—the Void of Impossible Things. Our Third Iteration was the creation of our home and our consequential banishment from the other Realm. This Iteration was both the longest and the most challenging—our mistakes had set off a chain reaction. My former body—Life—upon expelling the rest of its energy had given birth to a magnitude of souls. There were animals and creatures that walked the Earth and shook it to its core. Massive beings and fauna larger than anything that exists today covered the face of the planet. They walked among us here, too, massive majestic beasts we called the Ancient Ones. We soon lost control after long enough, and Father and I elected to end the Third Iteration together, and we decided to create the First Family along with the Fourth Iteration."

He stared at the familiar-looking shapes that appeared on the still water, and rather absent-mindedly, Davias repeated, "The First Family?"

"The First Family, Davias, was created to help us through the challenges introduced during the Third Iteration."

"What kind of challenges?" he repeated her again.

"When my energy was expelled and the souls were born—the Balance was tumultuously disturbed. The trillions of souls that were introduced had to be cycled between this Realm and the other due to the extreme lack of resources for all of them. And because they came from my raw energy, these souls were here to stay. Father and I struggled to organize and make the dichotomy between Realms work efficiently. So it was together that we elected to create the First Family and try again on what we thought would be the last Iteration. The Family helped—everyone found their place and learned their roles. We managed as a group for a while. In all reality, the Fourth Iteration could have and would have been successful were it not for the greed and the selfishness of you children. There were five of you, and an odd number meant there wasn't any balance. The Thinker, the Watcher, the Hunter, the Tamer, and the Weakest was Helena. You were one of these children, Davias—the kids called you the Thinker due to your . . . abilities." Mother finally paused, and the moving scenes reflected on the liquid surface stopped with her. She inhaled slowly, selecting her next words with extreme care. The images fluttered back to life as she spoke. "There were transgressions. Every single one of you held some responsibility. So, because of everything, Father and I reluctantly made a couple of difficult decisions. That is what brings us here—to the Fifth Iteration. One of the decisions that we agreed upon was to balance you and your siblings and to separate all of you as much as we can; for reasons I hope you'll never come to learn; this was what was decided would be the best for you. I'm sorry if you feel con-scripted to an existence or a purpose that is not genuinely yours to experience, but I promise you, my son, that your existence will have more excitement and purpose than any of your siblings. For now, though, you need to stay with me and learn. Tend to the souls and the tasks before the two of us." Above the two of them, a winged horse-looking creature let out a joyful cry as it soared high above the tree's canopy.

Mother took Davias by the hand and led the two of them away from the River Styx as the ferry carrying four of his siblings and a troop of souls ventured further out of sight and closer towards the Void of Impossible Things.

CHAPTER 3

THE RIVER STYX

The golden gondola peacefully split the river's water as it dutifully drifted on down towards the Void of Impossible Things. The river reflected a soft, yellow light from the edge of the boat, shining through the clear currents. The craft was at full capacity—Eliza and her twin Elias stood in matching positions at the helm, wearing their raggedy clothes. Together, along with Madrina and the Hunter, they overlooked the modest group of souls that joined them aboard. The four siblings each kept to their own business, except for Elias and Eliza, who exchanged communicative glances with each other as they dipped and dragged their oars in the water, continuously steering the boat down the river. The Hunter stayed at one end of the boat with his arms crossed and his feet dangling over the edge, while Madrina intentionally took to the opposite side, carefully cradling the blue soul in her arms. Her silky strands of hair draped down as she peered intently at the orb. Every so often, she would chance a look towards the shimmering wall of light that separated the Pre-Life from the Void of Impossible Things. She clutched the soul a little tighter and steeled herself for the first domino in such a vast chain of events, every single defining moment of which was already being spelled out inside of her mind's eye.

As unceremoniously as she could, she leaned over the edge of the boat near where Eliza stood paddling. As Madrina peered over the edge, she saw into the clear waters. Eliza looked at her and remarked, "When I stare into the stream, I can see all of you, individually. I can see anybody I want to. Elias can, too. Right now, I see this boat and all of us. I can even see Helena in the After-Life, and Davias is in the Pre-Life." This drew the attention of the brothers who moved a bit closer and stared as Madrina proceeded by dunking the soul into the River Styx. The Hunter got up from where he was perched and shambled across the narrow craft to observe his sister in tandem with the twins. Through the invisibly transparent water, the four siblings watched the soul pulse with different shades of blue until the color faded entirely to white, and the pulsing had subsided to a consistent glow. The white light remained around the small ball until Madrina retrieved it from the water, and it immediately regained its original blue hue—if anything had changed, the color had intensified to a far more vibrant shade. The light it gave off was brighter.

The Hunter clicked his tongue in feigned disinterest as he tried to reposition himself back in his previous spot with his legs dangling over the edge. Madrina didn't hear or see anything from the twins that indicated any interest in what she had done, so she breathed a sigh of relief to herself while hiding in the serenity of her eyelids.

All was quiet for a few moments until an annoyed voice broke the stillness. "Does Father know what you're up to?" the Hunter made her jump with his surprisingly harsh voice.

Madrina just rolled her eyes as she clutched the soul tighter to her breast. "Don't pretend that you have any idea of what is going on."

"What do you want from me? To match your audacity with ferocity? You think I'm just some animal begotten by Darkness and lost to madness? Do you want me to attack that soul in your arms?" he growled. His voice had lost the annoying tone as his pitch dropped lower. "You think I'm stupid, don't you? Just because I'm not the Thinker doesn't mean that I can't think for myself!" he added after another moment.

Madrina didn't move a muscle. She kept her focus and her wit about her as she retorted towards her obnoxious little brother. "You are so insecure. I mean, you could try that. Or you could sit back and continue to mind your own damn business while we each get our free ride. Don't ruin a good thing, Hunter." Hunter did not appreciate this at all as he crossed his arms and harrumphed back to his own corner staring into the water.

Then, he doubled back around and crawled back to his feet with a finger shaking in front of him. He bellowed, "Do you even know what you're supposed to do?" Madrina laughed in his frustrated face as she batted the finger out of her own.

"Just because I'm not designed to reap Human souls like you doesn't mean I don't have a purpose. What that purpose is remains up to my determination and requires no immediate instruction on your part. So, if you don't mind, you stick to what makes you tick, and I'll figure it out for myself."

The Hunter sneered in response. He pulled his head back and whipped it from side to side in forced amusement. "You're jealous of me, aren't you?"

"Why would I be jealous of you? Better yet, should I be?" Madrina exchanged her brother's condescending look with a dirty stare of her own meant to bring down his ego. The two twins exchanged looks of their own, silently trying to stay out of this sibling squabble.

Instead, the Hunter puffed his chest and pointed towards his angled jaw and beamed. "You want to be able to reap souls, just like me, don't you? You want the power between Life and death." He snapped his fingers, and charcoal-black particles began flaking off his skin and dissipating into nothing. "You want power at your fingertips." He took a step towards his sister, shortening the gap between them by half.

"Have you considered that I might already have that? The power between Life and death. Or are you so conceited you think that you're allowed to be wickedly unbalanced?" she retorted, and this time her words struck a chord. She dug her heels in and continued. She pointed at the group of souls that had congregated around her with one hand, while holding the blue soul close to her with the other. "The only difference between them and us is our ability to see and know existence for what it is. On our plane, you and I are the same."

Hunter jammed two fingers into his sister's chest, frustrated. "If that were true then you'd know about Mother and Father fighting. The Universe shaking. You would know about the Fourth Iteration."

"And how is it you remember anything about the fighting? I thought your memory got wiped, *Hunter!*" Madrina aggressively enunciated her final word as if it were punctuation. The Hunter powered up his other fist and leaned forward—black smoke poured out of the surface of both of his hands, and he held them in front of him, ready to strike.

"I'm not your brother, you little—" With a nod from Eliza, Elias wrenched the paddle from the water and interjected by swatting the two of them apart with it. He batted them to their separate corners and scolded both.

"Cool it! As you've mentioned, there's been enough fighting in our Family already—do we really need to be instigating any more amongst ourselves? When we each have a job to do?"

"What's your job then, baby brother?" the Hunter maliciously taunted. Like a jab, Eli felt the sting of his eldest brother's words.

"Are you seriously asking me that while standing on my boat?"

"Our boat," Eliza corrected him.

Elias ignored his sister's words. Not because he wasn't listening, but because his rage had blinded his every sense. He held the oar upright by his side like a staff and stood in front of his twin, protecting her. "Disrespect either one of us like that again, Hunter, and you'll have to ask Father for passage. Not me and not Eliza. You will be on your own," his younger brother threatened him. "And as for you, Madrina, you speak like you're better than the rest of us. I don't like that. You may be the oldest here, but you said it yourself, we are equals. When we drop you off, you are also on your own, to do whatever you damn well please. Due to your arrogance, I'm dropping the two of you off in different places, otherwise you might start another war. You'd be wise to brace yourself as we enter the Void." He warned as he looked between his two older siblings and sternly returned to his spot, dropping the wooden oar back in the rushing water. Eliza silently watched the entire encounter as she dutifully steered the boat without stopping.

The craft rapidly approached the shimmering veil of the Void of Impossible Things as the water began to pick up in turbulence. Eliza looked over her shoulder to the group of souls that had huddled together tightly following the dramatic exchange between the siblings. Seeing this reminded Madrina to tighten her grip on the blue soul in her arms. "We'll see about that, Eli," Madrina huffed quietly. Elias replied to her attitude with an arched eyebrow and a silent glance towards his twin.

Eliza replied with a nod and returned her gaze forward, brushing away her matted hair as she smiled. Finally, she chimed in with her mousey voice. "I think it's great that we each have our positions to fill. It does make us all kind of like equals in a way. As long as we are all working towards the same goal," she trailed off because she could read on the Hunter's face that her words were not welcome.

He rolled his eyes. "You and I, we aren't equals, darling sister. And you're naïve to think you could ever be my equal. What you do is inconsequential compared to me. Eli does the exact same job as you, so in my opinion, you're completely superfluous and desperately unwanted."

"What's your problem? Are you afraid of me?" Eliza's grey hair bounced as she confronted her brother. "Are you afraid of Eli? Are you afraid of what we are capable of?"

"What you are capable of?" he mocked, "I am Death, Eliza. I am capable of far more than you two ever could be. You do not intimidate me, nor frighten me. Not now. Not ever. You and that measly little paddle could do me no harm, but if you wanted to teleport me somewhere I'm sure that could be a little fun. You want to go on and try?" Hunter cocked his head backwards and laughed in mocking amusement.

It was at that very moment the wooden ferry punched through the silver wall and continued floating along forward, coasting on a blanket of white emptiness, floating ethereally through the nothing. The change caused the boat to jolt, which sent the Hunter flying off of his feet. Everything was white, even the rippling water of the River Styx had turned murky and milky as its babbling intensified. All around them were layers and layers of different shades of white light. Now that they were inside of the Void, each of the small, circular souls began to levitate, and their colors intensified. One by one, they popped out of sight and disappeared off of the raft, until the only one remaining was the blue orb wrapped in Madrina's arms. Elias called this out the moment he noticed it.

"Hey!" he pointed with his oar as he pulled it out of the white, milky water. "Why is this one still here?" He nudged the edge of the sapphire body as Madrina pulled it in tighter to herself in order to protect it.

Madrina stroked the blue aura with one of her long, elegant fingers. "He's a Vessel. He's anchored to me until I drop him off and give him unto Life."

"He?" Eli repeated curiously. "Why do you need a Vessel, Madrina?"

Madrina ignored his question and hummed under her breath before talking, being careful to formulate her words without emotion or information. "Yes, this is a boy. He will grow up sad, neglected, and alone, but he will always be loved and looked out for. He will be named David Prince."

"Why do I know that name, Madrina?" Elias asked her very quietly and carefully, as if his words could break glass—his anger had collapsed into curiosity. Never before had he seen a Vessel. The Hunter scoffed at the display of collective hysteria.

"Well, I do have my secrets, Eli. Telling you, now that might just let you in on a little too much. Plus, there's the matter of trust; I don't know where that information is going to go or what you are going to do with it. Just know that what I am about to do is far more important than anything that you could imagine." She shot a look in the Hunter's direction.

"You know I'm going to keep my eye on you then, if you aren't going to tell me," Eli warned. He motioned to the edge of the boat. "I'll be watching, you know."

"That's why we call you the Watcher, little brother. Keep watching; you might actually see something worth it."

Elias was silent for several seconds before he hummed shortly to himself and snapped his fingers twice. True to his word, he sent his siblings away, one at a time; Madrina would land in California and head east after seeing to the blue soul's new home, and the Hunter would arrive in Atlanta and head west. While in the Void of Impossible Things, Elias somehow knew they were destined to meet somewhere in the middle.

CHAPTER 4

THE AFTER-LIFE

The After-Life's collection of barren expanses was separated modestly like islands by large bodies of sharp, jagged slates of obsidian that protruded from the surface like black knives stabbed into the dusty-red horizon. One of these black stones rose high above the rest like a tower near the edge of the After-Life itself. It dwarfed its surroundings and obscured the swaths of grey, colorless souls below in a dark and cold shadow.

Helena lazed on a small plateau atop this spire. She was lying on her side, propped up by her left elbow, her thick hair draped just as lazily as she was while she stared off in the direction of the Pre-Life, subtly obscured by the Void, her mind lost in a daydream. Her right wrist spun in tiny circles as she created great big boulders out of nothing and sent them hurtling over the edge of the After-Life only to be swallowed by the Void of Impossible Things. Meanwhile, below her, at the base of the towering black rock, a crowd of thousands of souls longed for her attention, desperate for their reincarnation. She blocked out their drowning hum with her daydreams until Father interrupted her thoughts, and she dropped a boulder beneath her accidentally. It crashed to the ground with a cratering impact, scattering a cloud of dust and souls.

"Helena!" Father bellowed angrily. Recovering from her brief fright, Helena rolled her eyes before crawling to the edge of her platform and peering over. Father stood at almost a quarter of the height of the tower. His head was craned up high, and he bashed one of his fists into the rock. His black beard rippled with his disapproval as his eyes furrowed deeply. "If you're not going to respect the Balance by destroying after you create then you shouldn't be creating," he scolded her directly.

"I'm not creating anything," she lied. "It's the same boulder again and again. I created it once. One time, and I threw it into the Void, and it disappeared as if it never existed, because guess what? Once it goes through the Void it never did exist. So when I create it again, it's as if I am making it for the first time."

Father breathed a huge sigh of disappointment. "That's not how this works, Helena. And how did this rock get so tall?"

"I was bored, and I wanted a place to lay down," she confessed without a second's hesitation. She rolled away from the edge and crawled to her feet. The moment she was upright she heard a snap, and the tower disappeared from underneath her. She plummeted through the air in a free fall until one of Father's gargantuan hands plucked her out of the air by her arm. He held her in place in front of him while he shouted.

"You were bored? While *thousands* of them were waiting for your attention? When we talked about our plans for building, we did not discuss a *tower*," his annoyance caused him to emphasize his final word before taking a deep breath and continuing. "Do you know how negligent you sound? How lazy you look and how arrogant you make me appear to them—to the rest of our Family? You'll do your job, you'll create only what and when I tell you to, and you will give passage to these souls when it is their turn. Do you understand?"

Helena scoffed and tried as hard as she could to avoid eye contact with Father. "There's better things to do," was all she mustered.

Again, he responded with a deep, disappointed sigh. "You are infuriatingly stubborn, my daughter. You will come to accept your role—eventually, even if it kills me. But for right now, let's just talk about your siblings. What are your plans for recruiting?" He placed her back on the ground, and she rotated her shoulder in an attempt to regain some comfort as the souls began to swarm her in the spot that Father had placed her down.

After beating a few of them away with the back of her sore arm, Helena looked up to Father's waiting face. "No plans," she announced confidently and quickly. "But I know what I have to do. I know my next steps."

"How do you intend—" Father began assertively. Helena interrupted him by holding up her good arm. She began speaking immediately.

"It's all about what each of them want; Davias is a lost cause; he just wants knowledge. I can't give him that, I don't want to give him that. Eli wants desperately to be off of that boat, and the Hunter simply wants power that he can't have. Not only do I know how both of those poor boys feel, but I can help both of them out of their misery and not only put them on our side, but allow us some semblance of control over the two of them. If we leverage Eli properly, we can use him to establish some dominance over Eliza—and if that doesn't work, we can always just kill her. I think I already know how to do that."

"Helena! You cannot talk about killing your own siblings with such disregard. We toiled too much to speak of such things. Creating you children was more work than you can understand. We are the Prospected Family. That means each of you has the prospect of eternal greatness and a lasting legacy. If you'd just do your damn jobs and stop making such a mess. You will come up with a different plan. One that doesn't involve murdering one of our own."

"If we can't have both Watchers on our side, then we might as well have a monopoly on the only one, right Father? I mean, after all, you've been fighting this war with Mother for how long? If you want the upper hand, sometimes you have to bring someone to their knees. You said we are bound for greatness, but where is yours, Father? Your biggest mistake in all of this, if I may speak so openly, has been respecting the Balance the way Mother wants you to. She's weaker than you are. I have been called the Weakest, but in reality that should be her title to bear, and to hide, she makes you respect the Balance. You limit yourself to appease her own burdens, and I am here to pull the wool off of your eyes, Father. Call them, call Eli and the Hunter here, and we can get to work."

"My greatness is supposed to be *you*. You are supposed to be my eternal legacy. Right now, you are acting like more of a disgrace than a daughter. If you want your brothers here, then you do it," he barked as he crossed his arms and made to walk away from Helena.

"How am I supposed to summon them? Isn't that your field of expertise, Father?" she cried after him as he strode away. Father stopped and turned backwards over his shoulder, then, after a heavy sigh, he turned back around and knelt low enough that he and Helena were practically face to face.

"Don't you already have a piece of Darkness that I gave to you? Use that extra energy. It's finite without my Essence, but you'll have enough. Send it through the Void," Father said softly then gently held up one of Helena's arms in front of both of them. To demonstrate, he pinched her wrist, her skin appeared to turn to ash and smoke rose up gently. It condensed as it coiled in the air, turning itself into a small diamond. Father plucked it out of the air, and with a flick of his fingers, he sent it shooting through the sky, darting into the Void. As soon as it was out of sight, a red lightning bolt ripped across the sky like a ribbon, and a violet sphere appeared in front of her. The sphere dissolved and revealed Eli who had both arms wrapped around the Hunter while holding onto his oar. The Hunter was fighting against his younger brother angrily but wasn't able to break his grip.

"No! No! Send me back!" the Hunter snarled angrily as smoke began to fume out of his eyes. "What am I doing back here?" Father walked over and separated the two of them while trying to avoid being struck. Father caught one of the Hunter's smoldering fists in his massive palm and retaliated with a punch of his own to the Hunter's chest, causing him to clutch his chest and double over in pain.

Father lifted his son's limp body with his massive arm. He brought him up by the back of his open vest to meet him face to face. He hung there, defeated and calm. As he spoke, he sprayed the Hunter with his spit. "You will have plenty of opportunities to hunt. But before you go, we need an opportunity to talk without Mother being able to listen. You will go back when we tell Elias to take you, and you go where he sends you. Elias, do you know if your sister is watching us?"

"Not likely, but I can't be sure. Without me, she's on her own to gather the next souls," Eli quietly answered. His hands were crossed gently behind his back, holding his oar which stood up tall behind him. "I just told her I had to help you with an errand."

He was less angry, and he took another deep breath. "That's good. At least one of you is obedient, but that was always like you, Elias. We have work to do, the four of us, and we will need to work together. I'm not talking about our usual duties. This is something different. What we do needs to be done with discretion and without question," Father glanced between his two present sons and then towards his daughter. "We're building something. Helena, did you want to explain?"

"I—uh . . ." she stuttered, "I'm not sure where to begin." Father tried his best to hide his frustration as he continued.

"Our reality, as a Family, is and always has been one of . . . disharmony. You boys don't need to be bothered with the history or the semantics of everything at this time. If you come to remember details on your own terms, that's fine, but I want all four of us to focus on the right now with keen attention to what lies in front of each of you."

The Hunter, still antagonized by his humiliation dealt at the hands of Father, sneered with an obnoxious tone. "What exactly lies in front of us?"

"Hunter, you have the ability to reap souls, and with that comes your role in keeping the Balance. As Eli demonstrated, not only does he watch you, but he is responsible for your transportation. I've already spoken with Helena about my expectations regarding her duties here, but your second expectation, daughter of mine, is to be the bearer of Darkness and all of its might for the ages to come. You each play multiple parts in this game. I am sure you know that our resources are not only limited, but they are challenged."

"Challenged, Father? By who?" Elias spoke up again, breaking the silence for his siblings.

"By Mother, your twin, Eliza, and the other two," he grumbled. "Our foothold in reality is at stake. We've had to create the Family twice now due to a distinct lack of obedience. So here we are at the Fifth Iteration—our masterpiece. All the while, Helena remarks about killing your siblings as if it were absolutely nonconsequential. We each have our part to play, whether we want to or not. And if we are going to go toe-to-toe in a war with the rest of our Family, then we need to be smart in our approach so we can actually end this. I know what an existence of fighting will do to you. I want you kids to have the peace I never could, so if anyone has to die for it, it will be me—not one of my children. Helena, you said you had some ideas for your brothers.”

“Not just ideas, Father, but full-on plans. I lied to you earlier; I just didn’t feel like sharing,” she turned to her siblings, gesturing between the both of them and continued. “Now that I have a true audience, I’m more in the mood to share. I need the both of you on the ground in Life for a while to get some things done. In return, I will use the Darkness that Father has gifted me with to give unto you.”

The Hunter’s assertiveness melted away to greedy curiosity as he practically held his ashy hands out in front of him in order to receive. “What do you have for me, sister?”

“When you finally get around to your reaping, I need you to keep a steady supply coming here. As many as you can. It will keep Mother, Davias, and Eliza busy enough for us to move on to bigger things. In return, I will give you a second physical form— that of a crow. You’ll be quicker, stealthier, and more independent when travelling through Life.”

“And what do I get, Helena?” Elias asked modestly.

“You get the rest of the Darkness I have right now, so you can go create me a fortress. Build me a city and make it an empire. I want it in a place where the light never shines. Build me my sanctuary, my next queendom. You do this, and you get as much time as you need off of that boat,” she promised her youngest brother.

“Helena!” Father began to scold her once again. “My Darkness is not for your siblings—it is for you and you alone because you are isolated. You do not know the consequences of what could happen if Mother or one of the others get a hold of that Darkness. Second, you cannot take a Watcher off of the boat; it is his strict responsibility to see—”

“You took the Watcher off the boat, already. Let Eliza bear his burden; we want to gain and maintain the upper hand, correct?

Inundate Mother and Davias with a flux of reincarnating souls, and keep Eliza overwhelmed with the amount of ferrying she has to do solo, that'll leave Madrina on her own. You want me to build? Well, I want a Watcher."

"Madrina's already in Life, doing . . . something," Eli confessed. "We took her there already. She created a Vessel, or at least that's what she called it. She said his name was David Prince."

"What is she doing there, little brother?" Helena cooed. "What is a Vessel?"

"I have absolutely no idea. I only took her there, and she vanished the moment we broke out of the Void."

Father looked at his own feet with a hand clasped around his mouth. He spoke with a downcast tone. "If they have a Vessel then it means Mother's plans are already in motion. Don't be fooled, kids. She may seem passive and peaceful but Mother has outwitted me at almost every turn in our history. Don't let your guards down."

Helena turned to her impatient brother and quickly commanded, "Then you have another job to perform, Hunter. A more important one. Track down Madrina and keep tabs on her. Make sure she isn't up to anything . . . diabolical, and if you can, either take her out of the equation or occupy her somehow. Reap the Vessel if you can."

"I can find out where she is and take him there," Eli offered, then added, "I know where to build your city, so I can get started on that when I am finished."

"Helena, you cannot take the Watcher off of the boat," Father warned again.

"I'll hold his place on the boat for as long as is needed," the Hunter offered, causing all heads to turn in his direction. "But, let me get to Life first, and begin that steady supply of souls for you, and when we are in position, I will head back to the boat, relieve Eli of his position, and from there, not only can I keep

Eliza occupied, but maybe I can learn more from her than you can, Eli."

"Are you insane? There isn't a thing Eliza wouldn't share with me," Eli defended, causing Father to intervene once more.

"Save it. There's plenty of hostility and anger to go around, but there is a place and a moment for these emotions. I'll agree to letting the Watcher leave the boat to build on your behalf, Helena. Give him the Darkness he needs. I trust the three of you *not* to let me down this time. Helena, you'll need to share your plans with me. Eli, you need to guard that Darkness with your very existence and use it only to create. While you are all busy with your responsibilities, I will try as hard as I can to keep the Balance."

"What happens when we are finished, Father?" Eli asked.

"This is not my design, boy. You'll have to ask Helena for her direction on this one."

"When we are finished, boys, you will meet me and Father here, and we will ascend to our final glory. In due time, we will find ourselves marching towards the Pre-Life. We will take the rest of the Family by surprise and bring them down!" On his departure, Elias snatched the hem of the Hunter's leather vest as he disappeared and dropped him to the location of his request—the same town Madrina was in.

CHAPTER 5

THE SIDES

A full moon illuminated the Midwestern summer night's sky with a ghostly sheet of soft, white light. The constellations pierced the atmosphere with extreme ease. A luscious green meadowland stretched out invitingly across a countryside, and it ran unobstructed as far as it could, right up to the edge of a lazily running creek. In the warmth and near-stillness of the night, the water seemed to clatter loudly between the muddy banks.

Madrina walked through this clearing confidently and slowly, letting the tall grass tickle the sides of her exposed legs. She walked barefoot so she could feel as connected as possible to the environment and her surroundings, still her skin showed no dirt or mire; she was as pristine as she was beautiful and elegant. Mixed in with her confidence as she walked was a grace unmatched by any other being on Earth, and she let this combination shine through her every feature.

Something inside of her tingled like electricity, though instead of a physical sensation, Madrina experienced it as more of an internalized feeling, like a strong instinct. She stopped walking and knelt down to the ground and placed both of her hands into the soil, and with a *poof*, a massive cloud of souls rose to the surface and hovered just a few inches above the grass. At the same time, a bright purple light lit up the nearby area as Eli's glass-like bubble appeared and then melted away leaving the Hunter alone in its wake.

"What are you doing here?" she cried at him the moment she realized who was approaching. He marched through the foliage, drying it up in his wake and leaving a trail of dead, brown grass behind him. He twirled floating ash through his fingers as it flaked off of his skin. His bare chest reflected the moonbeams dully, revealing a topography of musculature and smoldering, cracked skin.

He stopped walking and glanced around almost hungrily at the wide array of souls in front of them. "I'd like to thank you," he answered his sister in a tone just short of condescension. "Came to do my job for me?"

"I don't care about you or your job, Hunter, so why don't you just leave me alone please?"

The corners of his mouth curled as he sneered at his sister. "Aren't you supposed to be the compassionate one, Madrina? Saying you don't care about me doesn't seem all that compassionate, you know."

"Care and compassion are two very different sentiments, brother. But I don't expect you to know the difference. You're all about death and misery, fueled by the Darkness in you. I do have compassion for you, though. Do you want to know how I know? I pity you, through and through." She pursed her lips and stopped talking abruptly, leaving a silence that was desperate to be filled.

"Your pity disgusts me, but at the same time, I feel some pity for you as well. So maybe the disgust is just as mutual, no?" the Hunter said after a long, silent moment. He began to look from soul to soul out of the myriad that lingered between the two of them. "What are the souls for?"

"I don't need them actually; I was purifying the land. I was about to figure out what to do with them when you came along. So either your timing is perfectly coincidental, or someone was watching me."

"Well he is called the Watcher," the Hunter joked.

Madrina quickly tried to comprehend what her sibling had told her while her emotions did several backflips inside of her chest. "Eli was watching me?"

"He was told to drop me here," he corrected. This appeared to set Madrina on the edge of whatever emotions she was already teetering on.

"Told by whom? And I'm being watched, now? How long has that been going on for?" She dug one of her heels into the soil nervously. Consciously, she didn't want her nerves to show on the exterior, but at the same time, she couldn't help but react to what she was being told.

"I don't think you've fully grasped how little the concept of Time applies to us."

"How many times have you jumped the Void, little brother?"

"Three," Hunter tried to answer coolly as he gazed over the souls again, as if their presence was tantalizing him, calling his name cruelly.

"And you must think that is enough for you to know everything there is to know about Time. You hardly show this Universe—or the fundamental pieces that make it up—any respect. Do you even know when we are, or even where we are, Hunter?"

He scoffed in his own defense. "Like any of those details matter? We run this world; what difference does it make where or when we are?"

Madrina closed her eyes and kept them closed while she took a deep breath. She closed her eyes so that when she rolled them, her brother wouldn't overreact. When she opened her eyelids, she looked deep into his scraggly-looking face and replied. "No respect. Nope. None whatsoever. Just like I thought," she trailed off, murmuring under her breath.

"Do you know why I have zero respect, Madrina? It's because they are still fighting—we are still just pawns in an eternal struggle for power and leverage. I'd like to do my own thing, but I'm at everyone else's beck and call. *Just like you.*"

"Oh, I know," was all that Madrina replied with. She hummed to herself as she turned away from her brother and walked towards the creek.

"*You* know, and you're out here in the middle of nowhere, who knows when, doing nothing? What is it you even said you were doing?"

"Purifying land from the disgraces of Time in the middle of the nineteenth century in the countryside between Oklahoma and Missouri. If you want these souls so bad, you can take them; I'm tired of watching you drool over them like a dog." Try as she might to dismiss her brother's greed, she couldn't shake her own nerves.

Disregarding the insult, the Hunter began reaping each soul one by one with soft, but deliberate touches to each little circular cloud. His green eyes grew more and more acidic with each soul he plucked from the area, and Madrina watched him looking like a fool as he meandered through the cloud. "You look ridiculous," she remarked.

"I look ridiculous? You're the one that—you look just like Mother, talk about ridiculous," Hunter stammered his way through his insult.

Tauntingly, she twirled her hair in her finger while curtseying in his direction to mock him. "I think I look beautiful, Hunter, thank you very much. You can't change that, nothing will ever change how I look or how I feel. But we *can* change what happens next."

"And what happens next, Madrina?" the Hunter questioned softly, picking the last soul out of the group. When she did not answer him, he repeated himself, but this time he released his anger in a bloodthirsty roar, "WHAT HAPPENS NEXT, MADRINA!?" She chuckled innocently and tauntingly, blinking her eyes not in her brother's direction but towards the indistinct distance.

"I don't know what happens next; I can only tell you what happened before. I can tell you we can change the outcomes ahead of us."

"How?" he asked, sharply.

Her sarcastic tone faded quickly as this time she seemed to plead with him. "By not fighting. By not killing, or destroying. We need to respect the Balance, like we were told to do. Don't play into Father's game. If he's approached you already, then we need you to reconsider—"

"It wasn't Father who approached me—us, Eli and me. It was Helena who brought us together. I mean, Father was there. But this all felt orchestrated by Helena."

"Then you tell Helena to stop Father's games and to do her job. We all need to do our jobs."

"Is that what you're doing, sister? Or are you playing games, too?"

"You may not understand it now, but this *is* my job, brother. I am supposed to balance you and the destruction you will want to unleash upon this planet in the years to come. So go, be what it may—whether you lay waste to that which came before you or you walk on by like a wordless shadow, I will not stop you."

"We're coming for you. Helena wants us to build a bridge between the After-Life and the Pre-Life. You should either run or hide while you can." The Hunter harrumphed as he took up all of the remaining souls with a sweep of his arm, and in the same movement, his body darkened and folded in on itself—his feet shrunk into talons, his mouth pointed into a beak, and his skin and hair ruffled into black feathers as he took to the air in the form of a black crow. Surprised, but not entirely shocked, she spun on the spot as the bird circled her menacingly before breaking out of orbit. She watched him catch an updraft, and his wings took him far and fast. Madrina could have sworn she saw the bird's head turn towards her one last time before he ducked completely out of sight. She carried on her way, leaving a trail of bent grass behind her in the meadowland.

Madrina followed along the creek, lost deep in her thoughts while basking in the glow of the stale moon's light reflected off of the surface of the almost still waters. There wasn't a single sign of wildlife around—no flutter or movement, no twigs snapping in the distance. No birds to mar the clear, white sky. And though her thoughts wandered, she found herself stuck with the feeling that she still wasn't alone. She stopped, and moved towards the water's muddy bank, and dipped her hand in the wet soil, feeling the grime and silt on her delicate skin, and she felt connected— she cared for this land, she longed for it to make sense, and she wished for it to be so much more than it already was.

Loneliness—to Madrina—was more than just a feeling. She lived loneliness through an existence of exile and isolation. She knew that she had been blessed with something her siblings did not have, and so it was born within this loneliness her urge—an ambition to bring to Life that which did not already exist.

Her ambition to bring new to Life and her wish for this land to make more sense to her gave way to a desperation. A pit in the bottom of her stomach that quickly rotted her away from the inside when movement in a small clearing of grass a dozen yards away from her caught her eye.

Carefully, she began advancing towards it as a swell of emotions flurried within her—anticipation, curiosity, fear, hope, and dread poisoned her nerves. As she drew nearer, she steeled herself to speak, to say anything, and so her lips stuttered, "Hunt— Hunter?" But when she approached the small clearing every ounce of her emotions had turned to surprise to see Davias, her other brother, instead. He was lying on his back with his hands resting underneath his head.

"What are you doing here?" she shouted at him. "You scared me!"

He used one of his tucked hands to wave at her and smiled in the pale night's light. "Why did you think I was the Hunter?"

Her surprise quickly soured to frustration, as she wasn't entirely ready for another conversation despite the loneliness that she felt she wallowed in. "Because he was here—why are you here?"

"I'm here to check on the investment. Mother sent me, and Eliza brought me in secret," Davias said with a flat tone while pointing directly into the star speckled sky. "Is that where you think they are in relation to us right now?"

"They aren't up there, Davias. You know what is up above us—millions and millions of planetary bodies that Mother created in the First Iteration. *Where* the Pre-Life and the After-Life are is not relevant, nor will it ever be."

"How do you know what happened in the previous Iterations? Mother's only barely told me."

"I have my ways, Davias," Madrina joined him on her back in the clearing. "And, as you said, the 'investment' is safe and secured."

Davias was quiet for a moment as he traced the stars burning in the night sky with his finger while humming uncertainly to himself. "Where?" he finally asked—just the one word.

Madrina tried her best to quickly downplay his question, "Why do you need to know? Telling you jeopardizes the security of—"

"Just tell me where on Earth it is," he demanded, then he corrected himself. "Where *he* is."

"I'm not telling. I'm being *watched*, Davias."

Davias sat up from where he was and didn't turn to look at his sister. He brushed off the dirt and dust from his clothing and walked himself to the water's edge. He spoke out over the creek, as he spoke to his sister behind him. He knew she could hear him, but whether or not she was listening, he was unsure. Something inside told him she was. "We need you. And we need you to not be ignorant or naïve. If you know anything about the early Iterations then you know who and what we face, whenever we get to facing that ugliness. Don't be a fool. Don't be a hero, or a martyr. Just do what you're supposed to do, and we'll all get by just fine."

There was a deafening silence between the two of them once he finished speaking. It was so eerily quiet that he had to glance over his shoulder to ensure his sister was still there. She was standing in the small clearing, yards off. Her already pale features were brightened in the moonlight as if she were made of porcelain.

"California—he's in California," she relented softly. Then he heard her take a deep breath and continue with a little more confidence. "Hunter was here before you, like I said. Not that his presence means anything to me—he doesn't. What bothers me is the fact that the two of you were so quick to approach me as if you wanted nothing to do with me, but you wanted everything to do with what I had to offer. You both used me, and in both situations, it would have hurt less if one of you had simply just asked me beforehand, instead of subtly manipulating me; that's not something I will forget, Davias. But every single one of us in this Family knows nothing but greed and selfishness. So you ask me not to be ignorant, but have you asked the rest, or have you stopped and asked yourself to shelve your ignorance for a moment? That's why we're still fighting, brother. I'm not being a fool by having my guard up, and how dare you think I want to be a hero! I'm alone out here. This is depressing, but I put in the work because it needs to be done. I let Hunter push me around because I get nothing out of fighting him. So maybe that's something you and the rest of them can learn: that you get nothing out of fighting with one another."

Davias remained turned away from Madrina, but his head was looking over his shoulder, so he straightened his body to square up with her and tried to make eye contact, though she did her best to avoid him. He gave up after a few seconds and said, "Perhaps, if we didn't have as many secrets then we could actually begin to rely on one another. Perhaps communication is better than selfishness—but you know every one of us has our secrets. You have yours, and I have mine—that's what drives our family's greed. And the lies we tell each other are the walls we use to keep our secrets safe. The lies we tell ourselves are the ones that betray us the most. So I want you to stop fighting me—stop lying to yourself and help us."

Wordlessly, Madrina joined him at the creek's edge and pulled her brother into a one-armed side embrace while the two of them looked at their reflection on the surface of the water. "If I tell you my secrets, brother, that means you need to tell me yours. So I want you to tell me what you know about the First Family. What has Mother mentioned? You answer that for me, and I will tell you where the Vessel is in California."

"You want to know about the First Family? Fine, easy enough. Mother and Father and the five of us: The Watcher, the Hunter, the Tamer, the Weakest, and the Thinker. I was the Thinker. Helena was the Weakest. We know who the Watcher is, that was Elias, and Hunter speaks for himself. I have no clue who the Tamer was, though. From what Mother told me and from what I understand, the Fifth Iteration was a punishment—they had to reprimand all of us for something that we played a part in. That's all I really know, though I have some empty-handed theories on what had happened."

Madrina looked solemn, as if she wanted to be frustrated but had neither the energy nor fortitude for it. "You don't know what it was Helena did or what the specific punishment was?"

"I told you what I know, honestly. Now, please," he begged.

Madrina put her hands on her hips and cocked her waist to the side in a pouting stance. "I'll uphold my end of the bargain and give up the exact location, Davias. But, keeping true to my word, I will not tell you where he is. I will show you and Mother and those we can trust, but now is not ideal, as I am sure you understand. I need to be here, with this land. I cannot explain it to you right now, as I do not fully understand why myself. But my instincts lead me here. My Life leads me here. Do you understand?" Davias nodded his head. "Good," Madrina muttered. "Now let's call Eliza and get you back home. I have much more work to do here. I will call her and head home behind you shortly."

Davias raised one of his hands to the sky and gave his ring finger a snap and in a massive flash of blinding pink light, Eliza appeared atop the golden gondola in the creek before their eyes. Davias scrambled through the muddy water to climb on top of the boat, and with a wave exchanged between him and Madrina, Eliza dipped her oar in the water, and they disappeared as the River Styx and the Void of Impossible Things folded away from view. "I'll be right behind . . ." she trailed off as they faded from sight. "You . . ." she softly finished once she was alone.

Once again, like the bitter, cold sting of the Midwestern air, the loneliness that had accompanied Madrina for quite a while settled back in. She grabbed at a bunch of the silk gown draped around her and continued barefoot through the meadow once more as her skin began to glow with a soft white light.

CHAPTER 6

THE WEAKEST

Helena trudged her way through the dust towards Father, who stood alone on the flat slats of obsidian that jutted out near the edge of the After-Life. A large swath of souls crowded around him as he prepared each one individually for their return to Life. When he sensed his daughter's arrival, he looked up from his business and scowled at her immediately. "Where have you been? What have you been doing? Do you realize how long you've stuck me with doing *your* duties?"

Her eyes rolled into the back of her head as she dug one of her heels into the dirt. "I've been exploring—learning more about what this place has to offer."

"And what does it have to offer you, Helena?" Father scolded sarcastically, but Helena missed the rhetorical nature of his question.

"Aside from millions upon millions of lousy mortal souls waiting for a second chance at Life, you have a small arsenal of Ancient creatures that I would love to get my hands upon. Several blood-thirsty beasts waiting to take a walk."

"They have nothing to do with you! Keep away from them, please, Helena," Father quickly lost his attitude as he pled with her. "Now come over here and help me with these." One by one, Father was restoring color to the shapeless forms as they floated through the ether towards Mother and Davias, waiting on the other side of the Void of Impossible Things.

"And why are there so many?" she continued, absent-mindedly.

"You told your brother to reap to his heart's content, to keep the rest of the Family busy, remember? Did you not stop to think about the repercussions it would force upon us as well? You didn't stop to consider yourself in the equation. You're neglecting the Balance, Helena. It's almost like you want to do nothing."

"But . . ." she began, but forced herself to stop, which caused one of Father's eyebrows to arch.

"Go on," he coerced, gently but firmly. A thick silence fell between them, one that was tangible and blanketed the overall air with awkwardness and mutual tension.

"We are doing nothing, Father. *You* are doing nothing while Mother and her merry band of my siblings sneak away and plot and scheme against us. You know they are conspiring against us—Eli has all but assured us of that, and yet you ask me to keep on like absolutely nothing has changed!"

Father continued restoring each soul, individually by hand, while trying to make eye contact with Helena, but she made every effort to avoid looking at him directly. "So what can we change? What can we do to tip the scales in our favor at this time? I figure you have an idea—or you wouldn't be sitting around so purposefully; that would be too damaging to your pride."

"I do have an idea—but I need you to tell me more information first," she finally levelled with Father.

"You finally come to me with a request. A request cloaked behind a hidden agenda, I feel. Perhaps you're keeping some secrets, child of mine? Be careful with that; you and I need to work together."

Taking a deep breath, Helena spoke quickly, but loudly. "Well, I am not the only one with a secret—nor a hidden agenda, and that's what I have to ask you about, actually. Can you tell me what you know about Vessels?" she bolstered her voice with confidence. Her attempt to win Father over on charisma alone fell flat when he responded. "I'm assuming you'd know all about them."

"Come over here and help me send these souls off. Then I'll tell you everything you need to know. How's that for an exchange?" So with plenty of huffing and pouting, after she realized that she had hardly a leg to stand on, Helena finally gave up her resistance and tended to the souls, taking them one at a time in both of her hands. She hated everything about the souls—the sounds they made, the way they looked, the way they felt like gelatinous air being squished around in her hands when she had to lift them. She especially didn't like the way they squirmed and hopped around in her grasp when she finished the restoration. Unceremoniously, she tossed each one over her shoulders when she was finished with them, and the souls would glide and float happily through the air. Helena sped through the crowd before her and Father. When they were finished, another awkward silence fell between the two of them, both of them expecting the other to speak first.

Father walked away after a long moment, waving for Helena to follow after him as he did. They marched across the slabs of black rocks and hiked around some of Helena's leftover boulders that she created and dropped onto the landscape, but it didn't take long for the two of them to come to a completely flat clearing in the rocks and the dirt.

"You say we are doing nothing—and yet, you have sent your brothers off with separate purposes, yes?" Helena nodded in response to Father's question. "And it is my understanding you want *me* to do more in the present, is that also correct?" Again, she nodded. "The fact that Mother and your other siblings have secrets and they are keeping them from you upsets you, too. So you can understand my frustration and my anger when I see you keeping secrets, laying out hidden agendas, and neglecting what you need to do to maintain the Balance."

"I do not understand your infatuation with—"

He didn't even give her the opportunity to complete her sentence before cutting her off by holding up one of his massive palms to her face. "Maintaining the Balance between everything in the Universe is how we convince the others we aren't up to anything. It is also how we inherit our power from the Darkness—no Balance leads to less power. The moment the scales tip and we are to blame, every eye will turn to us, and they will know we are up to something, and we will pay the price for it. I want you to trust my experience on this matter because I have learned this lesson firsthand. You think I ultimately care what happens in Life? No. I don't care at all; I never have. So long as I get what I want, when I want it. And in order to do that, I have to do just a little work sometimes—the bare minimum—to keep things just the way I want them. So you would be wise to do the same, or everything that keeps you and me safe and secure will come crumbling down in a dazzling display of futile attempts and ultimate, bitter, stinging failure. Failure is built on mistakes!" He shouted, then he pursed his lips sternly and breathed heavily through flared nostrils. "You've made one mistake, and that is assuming I do not have anything planned. First, I want you to build me a proper tower, a tall standing observatory where we can speak away from any interruptions or distractions. Anoint us both with the thrones we deserve. Do this, and I will tell you what you need to know about Vessels after we gather your brothers. You see Helena, I still hold a hand over you, my daughter. So long as you need to ask me questions, you will need to learn to respect me and my expectations."

Helena felt the Darkness she had inside stir. She tensed her muscles with rage and wrenched her arms up towards the sky as if attempting to lift some invisible, incredible weight. First, her knees began to buckle under the pressure, then her skin began to turn red, spreading from her fingers up her arms. Bright red streaks ran through her hair as she slowly began to rise with the bedrock beneath her in tow. She spun and twisted her arms around, making elaborate, geometric shapes in the air as the rocks seemed to melt around them, encasing them in a molten bubble. Upwards they went until they towered over the land, lording over their dominion and the millions of souls beneath them. With a final wave of her hands, Helena tore open a walkway outwards, creating a magnificent balcony out of nothing but melted, dripping obsidian that was hardening into blackened stalactites. She closed her eyes, and with a snap of her fingers, Eli appeared instantly, as if he was summoned against his will, holding his oar upright directly by his side.

"Go and fetch the Hunter once more. It seems that we have more to discuss amongst us," she commanded, looking not at Eli but in Father's direction. The Watcher understood, and with a single tap of his oar against the ground, he was gone for a mere second before returning with his older brother, who sat in his bird form perched upon the Watcher's shoulder. The Hunter took flight briefly before resuming his normal appearance, landing on the ground in a neat glide beside his brother. The two of them admired the tower room for a few moments before turning their attention towards Father and Helena.

"You want to know more about Vessels? Let me first start by asking if any of you even remember what happened in the Fourth Iteration. The First Family? The Tamer?" When three shaking heads told him that what he was saying didn't resonate with his children, he continued. "We are different from *them*," he was pointing below him, alluding to the souls of the dead. "Vessels allow you to *become* one of them, to inhabit a mortal frame. It is also an effective method of hiding from another one of us—unless one of us knows who or where you are, you'd be lost in a world of billions of mortals."

"Have you ever been Vesselled, Father?" Helena took an opportunity to interrupt with a question.

"Never—I cannot be Vesselled; only you and your siblings can. We are not quite cut from the same cloth. You're woven with Time. I am not so I cannot leave this Realm—not anymore. But any of you can, and it is my belief that Mother is going to try to use that Vessel against us in some way."

Helena pointed to Elias. "We already have a Watcher. What does a watchtower have anything to do with countering a Vessel? I'm not following," Helena whined, but Father held up a finger to order her silence.

"Being inside of a Vessel traps you; it strips you of any powers. Most importantly, being Vesselled will actually make you mortal. This means when your Vessel dies, you won't transcend the Void and return home. Your existence will cease. The only way to escape a Vessel is by being ripped out. Tearing your Essence from the mortal frame. This kills the Vessel. The only one that can do that is you, Hunter. So this watchtower, my sweet daughter, provides you protection. Both you and the Hunter."

"Protection from what?" they asked in unison.

Father puffed up his chest and began speaking swiftly and with authority. "Helena, you mentioned before that you knew there were Ancient Souls locked away here. Some that you'd like to get your hands on. There are vicious, ancient beasts here, right underneath us, that can, with enough effort, kill you and your siblings, too. There are more beasts, in the Pre-Life, and Mother will use them against us. Hunter, I don't want you aimlessly wandering around outside of this Realm anymore, unless you are monitoring that Vessel. No more field trips with Eli to

Life. And there's nothing that connects us to the Pre-Life, so you will be stuck here. You'll follow strict orders that come from me. Helena, if you won't do your primary duties, then perhaps your other talents can be of use. Elias, my youngest son, I have not forgotten about you. We need you back on that boat. You need to continue being our spy. You are named the Watcher for a reason. Listen and eavesdrop on as much as you can and report it back to us. That is, if you still choose to align yourself on this side, our side." Father stopped speaking abruptly. The silence came as a deafening *boom*, and all eyes shifted towards the Watcher.

Eli fidgeted in place with his free hand while his other hand tightened its grip on the long, wooden oar that he held upright. He responded with a wordless nod, and looked towards Helena who beckoned him to her with one finger curling into her fist. He approached her slowly and leaned in cautiously when she began to whisper.

"Before you go—I want to see the Vessel, and I want to see the city that you're building for me." Eli nodded in understanding and Helena grabbed his hand as she glanced over her shoulder—but Father reached out and tightened his massive hand in a clenched fist held high over his head. Ethereal black ropes made from shadow bound the two siblings before they could depart.

"Did you not just hear me say you need protecting? You will do no such thing!" He spat as he stood as tall as he could, filling his chest with the echoes of a thousand, million voices. "I am neither deaf nor a fool! Your commitment is to this Realm, not some forsaken city on the edge of reality. Don't let yourself be distracted by *Life*, Helena. Darkness calls both of us to rise and rule over this Realm with an iron fist!" Father's annoyed voice thundered loud enough to fill the newly furnished throne room with dread overcome with lasting authority. Helena reluctantly released her younger sibling's grip and rolled her eyes in Father's direction. Father continued, with a last minute change of course. "Eli—you will return to the River Styx on the ferry, like I said. You will keep an eye on the comings and goings from the other side and an ear on the words and whispers coming from our other half. I've decided instead, that the Hunter will remain in California for as long as he can in order to monitor the Vessel that Mother thinks she can hide from us. Eli, it is important that you keep an eye on the Hunter, make sure he remains safe. Your vigilance will be our truest protection. And lastly, Helena, you clearly need to learn more about what it is we do here and how to fall in line, so I want you to turn this watchtower into a castle. Then, we can talk about this bridge you are going to build. Until then, the Darkness will remain mine until you prove you deserve it."

CHAPTER 7

THE HUMAN

Madrina waited patiently on the boat with Elias and Eliza. Both of the twins were taking turns rowing and then staring into the reflective surface. They had just emerged from the silver veil that separated the Void from the Pre-Life and the River Styx. A larger-than-usual cloud of souls meandered in the middle of the craft, and a soft smile crept across Madrina's exhausted face—after working restlessly in the Oklahoman countryside for so long, she was finally able to return home and follow through on her promise to Davias. She watched the invisible current rush past the three of them as they drifted upstream. Ahead, near the shoreline in the distance, another bundle of souls flew around happily, like puffy little dragonflies chasing after each other. Below this buzzing swarm of souls stood two figures. Mother and Davias were poised stoically as they faced looking out over the shallow water towards the party arriving in the boat.

They pulled up to the golden shoreline near the towering Tree of Knowledge; the scenery was spotted with patches of shimmering, golden grass and various flora. The boat drifted gracefully, as if floating on a thin sheet of ice until it lodged itself on the bank. Madrina stepped over the edge and onto the terrain as she passed a wordless but affirming nod towards Mother, who stood still, dwarfing her and her siblings with her tall stature. Mother motioned for Eliza and her brother to leave the boat and join them with an open hand. The two of them silently obeyed as they carried their oars along with them. "Eli," Mother started when everyone was close enough, then paused and gathered her breath and her thoughts. "Thank you for joining us. Davias will be taking your sister's place on the River for a while. I'm sorry if this feels a little unexpected. Nothing else will change for now; you are still responsible for delivering our souls to their bodies in the proper time and place. In any case boys, I'd like to be very clear here; nothing else changes. Davias has been well-informed of what is expected of him and how to proceed. I will send Eliza to you, Davias, when it is time for you to return to me." She cast a solemn look in Davias' direction who took his cue. He stretched out his hand almost mechanically, reaching towards Eliza, who handed her oar off to her brother. With oar in hand, Davias shot one last look at Mother before turning to take his place on the ferry. The bundle of souls trailed behind him, as they took their places lining the sides of the small ship.

Eli took one look at his twin and weakly smiled before turning a stern face towards Mother as he announced, "I should inform you that I will also be taken off of the River. Temporarily. I'm not sure when, but Father has arranged for the Hunter to take my oar when we get to that point. I'll see you when we return," Eli tightened his grip on his oar and retreated without another word, placing the broad end in the water as he boarded. The ferry immediately lurched forward the moment that Eli had finished setting foot upon it.

As the boat began hastily drifting downstream, Mother turned to her two daughters, who now stood side by side in stark contrast: Eliza's rough and raggedy grey hair and pointed, mousey features dressed in ragged strands of cloth that barely hung on her bony body standing next to Madrina's waterfall of shining silver strands of hair and elegantly defined curves, hugged in the finest of white, silken garbs.

Eliza's face was smiling. Smiling from her first taste of freedom from the River Styx, but that smile quickly faded into a blank waiting expression as, once again, Mother paused in order to find her words.

"Eliza, it is certainly a pleasure to see you off of the boat. Finally," Mother announced with distinct pride in her voice, as if the two of them had pulled off something impossible together.

Eliza murmured quietly to herself before she found her words. "You know I don't mind being out there—on the River—right? But I like this, too. Being here, with you."

"I know, my dear," Mother began curtly. "There's some things we need to go over with you." Mother and Madrina exchanged nervous looks—their identical blue eyes locked for the briefest of moments before breaking away and focusing back on the youngest sibling.

Defiantly, perhaps because she noticed the exchanged glance, Eliza asked, "Then why am I here?"

Mother gestured to Madrina with an open palm. "We are in need of you and your position."

This put Eliza on the immediate defensive. "What do you mean?"

Mother began to explain, slowly and quietly. Madrina watched the two of them from the side. "The current arrangement is that you and your twin brother are the first points of contact for anyone going into or out of our Realm, correct? And you're both the only ones who can watch through the waters."

"That's right," Eliza bobbed her head cautiously, her bushy light brown hair bounced in return.

"That wasn't always the case, though. Did you know that there used to be just one of you doing the job you two are doing? That was Eli—your brother."

"I didn't know that, actually."

Madrina gave Mother a quick, surprised look. "I didn't know that, either," she chimed in.

"That's because you didn't exist either, Madrina. You're both newly conceived. We indeed had a family before you and your siblings as you all are now. There were five: four brothers and one sister. One was tasked with watching over the Pre-Life, the Thinker, gifted with unending knowledge and wisdom and powers of the mind. One was tasked with reaping the souls when they were due, the Hunter, able to weave through Time and space. One was tasked with ferrying souls to and from our Realm, the Watcher. The Tamer was the eldest and the only one able to control the Ancient Ones. The last was the Weakest, with the powers of creation and destruction. The Weakest . . . that's what the children called her.

"This Family was small, but they were meant to help us tend to the army of souls that we had created. With reason and order, we were able to maintain everything with a sense of stability. This stability gave us harmony and strengthened the resonating power that came from the Void. The Void's strengthening empowered each of us in turn in a reaction we came to refer to as the Balance. Thus, over the ages, the First Family's sole objective became maintaining the Balance. The Balance was kept by cycling the souls we created from Life to the After-Life, then from there to the Pre-Life, then back to Life, and the five of them did this well, but that was until the Weakest conspired against Father and myself and the rest of her siblings in order to try and become more controlling. Her rebellion was a catalyst to something more disastrous, however. With no souls coming into the Pre-Life, the Hunter decided he could and would flood the After-Life with a surge of souls so immense, Father and I did not know what to do. We struggled to find an agreeable solution. Father attempted to sway the Tamer to his favor in belief he could use his power to ferry a number of the larger, more Ancient Souls we have locked in the After-Life to Earth in order to make more room. I valiantly tried to keep the Tamer on course, and offered everything I could in order to have him working for me.

"Ultimately, the Tamer was manipulated and used by the Weakest, and the Hunter locked himself in Life with the Watcher, isolated from the rest of us since we could not voluntarily leave our Realm. Father fended for himself, as he could with the power of the Darkness, but I had to defend the Thinker, so when it came to it, I had to use some of my Life to protect him. He was innocent after all. It was then that Father and I realized that we had failed in our combined efforts, so we compromised by starting again and using Darkness and Life to cause another Iteration. This one with you and your siblings in mind, and better attention to the Balance. The Tamer was banished so he could never be used against the rest of us again and the remaining siblings had their memories reset. When the Family was redesigned, we had to make a few agreements. The first was that we must be balanced from within, so with the subtraction of the Tamer, that left one daughter and three sons. The decision here was clear. We needed two more daughters. Our next agreement was to keep the two of you Watchers as twins, divided and equal in order to keep the other in line, two bodies instead of one, so Father and I would not have to fight over that control, nor could anyone in the Family have total control. Madrina, you were created in order to help keep the Hunter balanced, one to take Life away, and one that can nurture it, and to provide the compassion and love that is absent from the Hunter's heart. You," she spoke to Eliza by extending one long, slender finger in her direction, "Madrina, and Helena. Three daughters. Elias, Davias, and the Hunter. Three sons. This time, we kept the Balance. Are you following so far?"

"So far I am, Mother, except I have one question. We are all named, but why does the Hunter not have a name?"

"He did, once. But he forsook it and chose to bear the title alone, and so for some while, we only used the titles the Family was given. He was named Mathias, but he did not want a name so similar to his brothers', and so he rebuked it. Now, you and your sister are here because you will both be playing special roles from here on out. Eliza, your brother just told us that he will be leaving the boat on Father's orders. This course of action is exactly what led us down the wrong path the last time, and we need you to stop it. You need to keep Elias on that boat as much as possible, prevent him from leaving his place. If at all possible, you need to stay by his side as often as you can. Additionally, I need you to be on alert for any mention of the name David Solomon Prince. Find him and watch him. I want as many pairs of eyes on him as possible at all times."

"David Prince. Who is that?"

"That is a Vessel. Our Vessel. A Human boy," Mother responded.

"Why do we need a Vessel, Mother? What is it for?"

Calmly, Mother looked between Madrina and Eliza and spoke softly as if explaining something obvious. "I fear, my daughters, that there may soon come a time when we will need to fight, and should the fighting fail for any reason, then you may need to hide. This Vessel—this Human helps us either way."

Eliza's voice began to reflect a hint of panic. "What makes you say all of this?"

"Father and Helena have something planned, this I was told by Madrina, who got the information from the Hunter. They're planning to build a bridge between the After-Life and the Pre-Life. If that's true, then they risk tearing a hole in the Void of Impossible Things. If that tear happens, we may never achieve the Balance again. Our only option at that point would be another Iteration, and I don't have a feeling that Father will cooperate this time to make that happen. So the line has been drawn, and our sides have been formed. I'm sorry Eliza, but Elias is the enemy."

"So what do I need to do? How can I help?"

"The Vessel is for the four of you to survive the fight, whenever it happens. You just need to make physical contact with him. Eliza, we need to find an opportunity for you to touch him. I may need Davias' continued assistance with figuring out how to accomplish that without tipping off your location to your siblings—or without giving away our intentions. Just so you know, only those of us who have touched a Vessel may enter it. Entering can only happen once. After that, it's sealed off."

Madrina interrupted her sister before Eliza had an opportunity to ask another simple question. "How do we do that, and what will happen to us when we do?"

Mother spoke directly towards Madrina. "You become anchored into that body by jumping into the water of the River Styx. Until you settle into the right timeline, you'll wander in the Void where anything can happen. You cannot return here until the body of your Vessel dies by the hands of one of us in the Family. If that happens, then you all will be set free, back to our Realm. As long as you are Vesselled, however, you will be locked out of our Realm; you will not be able to enter. If your Vessel dies a mortal death—a Human's death, you and your siblings, whoever is inhabiting that Vessel, will be lost and imprisoned forever."

"What will happen to you, Mother?" Eliza feared the worst. "Can't you come with us?"

"I cannot. I fear I am unable to Vessel myself, since I do not have Time woven into my being like you do. You need Time in order to pass through the Void. I will be fine, Eliza. I was, and am, and always have been. I fear nothing from Father, and even less from Helena. Their tactics and ambitions are highly anticipatory, and I am confident that I should be able to effectively counter them, especially with Davias' help. Now that the two of you are in your proper positions, I am doubly confident in our preparations."

"Mother, Hunter is already on some sort of warpath. He will likely stop at nothing to try and reap the Vessel. He's already stalked me out to Oklahoma. He's undoubtedly working an agenda for Helena. What prevents them from harming the Vessel?" Madrina raised a valid concern, reflecting back to her recent encounter with her brother in the American Midwest.

"That was Eli that escorted him to Oklahoma," Eliza confessed coldly to her sister, who growled in response. "I wasn't sure what was happening."

"Don't worry about that, Madrina. He would find himself incapable of doing such a thing. Vessels are complicated beings. To take a mortal soul and retrofit it so that it is not only capable of hosting one of our Essences but compatible with doing so and not perishing in the process takes significant power—in the form of Life. The energy that sustains that power and that capability comes from the Void of Impossible Things and, thus, through Time. In order to reap a Vessel—that is, in order to separate a Vessel's soul from its physical body before it is inhabited by one of us—that takes the full might of Darkness. You see, Darkness must undo what Life and Time brought together. Father may decide to imbue the Hunter with his Essence—the Darkness, but to be honest, I see Helena inheriting that power, and I don't see her sharing too much of it with her siblings once she has control. So, by the graciousness of Helena's greed, we may actually be safe from her wickedness. At least for a while," Mother's long-winded explanation was suddenly brought to an ominous closure. When she said nothing further, both Madrina and Eliza panicked together.

Madrina wasn't the first of the two to speak up, she was simply the louder one, so Mother didn't hear Eliza when she asked what they could do to buy more time. Instead, all she heard was a quick shout from Madrina. "How long is a while!?"

Mother hummed for a second or two before answering solemnly. "Hard to say with any sort of precision. Time progresses far differently between the two Realms. So what might feel like a short while here may take eons down there. Perhaps the opposite. What I do know is that our next steps are to establish who can use the Vessel, and this just comes down to which of you children have made physical contact with him. Madrina, you created the Vessel, so you have established that precedent already. Eliza, you and Davias still need to get that done."

Eliza quickly interrupted, "We could go now," thinking her proactivity would be helpful.

Mother responded with a scolding look. "Leaving the Pre-Life and the River Styx unattended. Strategically, it is not our best option. We need to wait it out for right now and find an ideal moment that won't upset the Balance—or any of your responsibilities." Eliza, having finally understood the gravity of the situation, nodded silently while maintaining eye contact with Mother.

"Eliza, before you return to the boat, bring Davias back here. As quick as you can, and take your place once more. Before you depart, however, I want you to wait for your brother and sister. It'll be a full raft again, I'm afraid, as they'll be accompanying the next group of souls to Life."

In a burst of a pink glass bubble, Eliza vanished from the spot and quickly reappeared with Davias holding her oar and standing by her side. Mother looked Eliza sternly in the eye once more and said the words "Be safe" before Eliza disappeared again after giving one final nod and taking her oar from her brother. Once the silence had settled back in, Mother ran her narrow, elegant fingers through her hair in mild frustration and turned to look at her son—her favorite son—and the daughter she had created in her image. His messy black hair and her neat, flowing white strands contrasted sharply with one another, but their smooth, pale skin and flawless, defined features showed their similarities.

"The two of you should know what we are about to face: Soon, if he hasn't decided to do so already, Father should be passing his Essence to Helena. His Essence—and mine for that matter—are different than that of you children. Your Essences are made up of Darkness, Life, and Time. His is pure Darkness, and once your sister has this, she will undoubtedly begin accelerating the assembly of that bridge in the distance." Mother motioned with the same fingers that had been fidgeting with her hair and pointed far in the distance. Faintly, through the mist and the Void's silver light was a faint outline of a rocky structure, ominously reaching towards the Pre-Life. It remained far from complete, but its visible presence began to spell unease with Mother.

"There's not a lot we can do to stop the construction of that bridge. So we need to make sure we are ready for when it is finished. Davias, I'll need your help figuring out how we are going to get you and Eliza to the Vessel without giving up our positions in the Pre-Life or the River Styx for longer than necessary. Madrina, this means I will need you to take the next ferry back to Rubidoux and watch over that child for us. Keep the Hunter as far away from that boy as you can manage. Take Davias to see the boy—but keep your distance unless you absolutely have to. Do you understand?"

"I will always be ready to fight for you, Mother," Davias said with only a hint of trepidation hiding in his voice. Madrina, however, raised a finger and a question.

"What I don't understand, Mother, is if Helena gets the Darkness from Father, and Darkness is what can harm our Vessel, then what is supposed to stop Helena from asking Eli to take her to David Prince and reaping him on the spot?"

Mother stared back at her daughter and half whispered the simplest response she could muster. "I just told you. *You* are supposed to stop Helena from reaping the Vessel. So go and do it."

CHAPTER 8

THE OFFER

A stream of colorful spools of immaterial clouds hastily hurled through the air, piercing through the transparent Void of Impossible Things as they departed Helena and Father in the After-Life and approached their destination: The Pre-Life. Mother stood with Davias as they usually did in the field underneath the Tree of Knowledge awaiting the arrival of the small troop. Madrina stood to the side with her long arms tucked gently behind her back while she observed silently. As if in sync with her thoughts, Mother called out to her softly, "Madrina, watch how we do this—the journey to Life begins here."

She motioned with her arms as the train of colorful souls rapidly approached, zipping through the air like ballistic projectiles. They slowed to a controlled hover and arranged themselves in a ring around the three of them in a ceremonious fashion. Mother stood still as Davias started with no soul in particular and reached out and held it in place with one hand. The other hand he placed gently on his chest, above his right lung, and he gently sighed as he began to see flashes of all sorts of different memories. Memories of good and bad, happiness, sadness, and anger. Recollections of loss, lies, lust, and loneliness flooded his delicate chest.

The feelings each left a lasting taste in his mouth. Some tasted sweet, while others filled his face with acidity. Every soul had different experiences, and not all of them filled him with terror and wrought. He found fondness in the more innocent souls they came across. Whichever was the case, however, he had to do the same process in turn with each and every being that departed the Pre-Life. After experiencing each of these memories himself, Davias took his own Essence and eradicated each memory and replaced them in turn. In their place, Davias beseeched new experiences of Life that have not happened yet and memories that have not yet been made. He did this with each awaiting soul in the circle until they were all washed from their previous existence and given their new destinies.

Madrina continued to watch silently as Mother then stepped forward and picked up and held each little orb in her arms, and the longer she held them the faster they spun, like rippling currents of air. She started walking past Madrina and walked towards the shoreline of the River Styx, and as she approached, the ferry appeared through the fog with both twins aboard, rowing the craft in perfect unison.

As the twins drifted nearer, the souls instinctively hopped out of Mother's arms and landed on the craft, safe and sound. They hummed and buzzed excitedly, as if knowing what the future held for each of them, and they were giggling with anticipation. Mother wordlessly nodded to Madrina and Davias, making stern eye contact with both of them as they boarded the boat with their siblings. As soon as everyone was in place, the twins pushed off from the shore in unison, and they began drifting away from Mother, who stood solemn and alone on the shoreline as she sent them off with a slow wave of her long arm.

None of the siblings uttered a word to another. Eliza was steering the craft while peering sharply over the edge while Elias stood still and stopped staring into the water. He quietly pulled his oar out and held it horizontally in both of his hands as he tentatively stared back and forth between his three siblings. He seemed tense and nervous before he disappeared in the blink of an eye, leaving behind a lavender cloud that clung to his spot for a second before he returned, bursting the lavender cloud with his body and bringing the Hunter along after him in the same purple bubble.

Madrina was quick to confront Eli. She got close enough to his face that the two of them could smell each other's breath. "What is *he* doing here? Why did you bring him?"

Unflinching and unafraid, Elias did not back down. He relinquished his grip on his oar as the Hunter took it from him, relishing the remarkable power he felt vibrating through his fingertips. Eli stood in his spot and straightened up to see Madrina eye-to-eye and responded coolly, defending his older brother to his immediate siblings. "I'm following Helena's orders—it's his duty to bring souls back to the ferry, Madrina, and it is my duty to see to the passage of those that need to come and go. So he's along for the ride under my protection, and you'll both get separate destinations, just like last time." Madrina harrumphed and removed herself from her brother's face, but not before she shot a nasty glare towards Hunter, who sneered back at her in return while twirling the oar between his blackening hands. Startled by the surprise encounter, the mass of souls condensed tightly in the center of the boat.

Madrina retreated closer to Eliza, and Davias followed suit, leaving the other two brothers alone together to conspire on the port side. Neither Watcher was watching. Hushed whispers and mumblings came from both groups, as the mass of neglected souls chirped and hummed mournfully. The boat quickly approached the silver border of the Void, and it was as if every sibling aboard noticed at the same moment. Eliza cast a glance directly towards her twin as he returned with a look of sincere sorrow. Just before the boat pierced the veil, without warning, Eli grabbed a hold of his paddle once more, and he and the Hunter disappeared in a bright purple bubble off of the ship. The other three didn't have any opportunity to react. They entered the Void of Impossible Things, and the three of them went their separate ways: Eliza stayed on the boat, because she knew she had to. Madrina went on to Rubidoux, California alone to watch the Vessel, and Davias was transported to a humid, moonlit cemetery, where he came face to face with his two brothers. The looks on their faces told him that they were expecting his arrival.

"What are you doing here? Where are we?" Davias asked, an audible hint of trepidation shook his voice.

"We were waiting for you, stupid brother. It's time to talk!" the Hunter cooed mockingly at Davias. He stepped forward and dismissed Elias with a wave of his hand. He disappeared quickly in his usual purple bubble, leaving behind a silence and a tension between the two brothers that only grew the longer they glared at each other. Davias cut the growing unease by responding as simply as he could.

"What could we possibly have to discuss between the two of us? Aren't you supposed to be . . . hunting?" Davias tried to retort sarcastically, but it came across flatter than he wanted it to.

"My job is to bring resources back. For Father. For the After-Life. *For our Family*. You have to understand; I want what's best for us."

"And what do you think is best for us, Hunter?" Davias tried to maintain eye contact, to maintain his composure and confidence. But it was Hunter who broke the gaze. He tossed his sight to the night sky and inhaled deeply through his nose, like he was smelling something strong.

"Dominion. Absolute control over everything, anything in Time and space. You name it, you got it."

"Do you not understand who you are, Hunter? Who we are, and where we come from? The things we can do; the powers we possess—"

The Hunter interrupted his younger sibling by stopping in his tracks and hoisting a smoking, blackened finger in his direction, "We!? *You*, dearest Davias, possess no powers. Helena can create material from nothing; I carry death in my palms. Eliza and Eli have free reign on travel, and we all know that Madrina has something hidden in her veins; I mean she's the carbon copy of Mother, is she not? I feel electricity when I stand next to her. But you, you do absolutely nothing. Davias, the Thinker. More like the 'Stinker.' So I have come to strike a deal. Make an offer. Bargain with you."

Davias scoffed, still trying his best to stare his brother down. "If you've come to offer me a 'place by your side' you can just leave. I won't have any Darkness. I won't have any part of your or Father's schemes. Did he put you up to this, or did Helena?"

"Neither. I'm here of my own volition because the two of them are too busy getting in each other's way to see the obvious. We can control the four corners: Life, the After-Life, the Pre-Life, and the Void—all we need is you by our side so we can capitalize on a presence in the Pre-Life."

"You didn't listen to a thing I just said to you, did you? The answer is no, I won't join you, Hunter. You're hardly the one to be making any offers."

"And why is that?" Hunter half-snarled, half barked. His skin turned ashy in a brief flare of his anger.

Davias laughed, which caused his brother to become even angrier, but before he could continue talking, Davias answered tartly, "Because you're an underling to an underling. Father is using Helena, and Helena is using you. You want to use me, and undoubtedly use Mother through me, am I right?"

The Hunter was silent for an extensive pause before he conceded under his breath. "You think you're so smart, don't you?" Not sure if he was meant to hear this comment, Davias pressed his luck, continuing to further his older brother's aggression.

"Yes, I do. They call me 'The Thinker' which means I know more than you, or Helena, or anyone else in this ignorant Family combined. You know what else I have? An actual *name*. You're stuck with your cute little title, but I actually have an identity. In the grand scheme of things, who do you think matters more? Me or you, Mathias?"

Hunter mockingly laughed angrily towards his younger brother while he lunged with both feet, taking off from the ground. He swooped into the air as he transformed into his crow form, and quickly camouflaged into the night's sky. Then, just as quickly, he darted out and came crashing down, landing back on his own two feet in front of Davias. His entire body flaked and dusted his landing with ash as the blackness once again made its way through Hunter's skin. With one hand he grasped Davias' left forearm tightly and held it firmly, preventing any escape as the power inside of him coursed with his pulsing anger. The Darkness began to rend and boil until the Hunter began to hear his brother's agonizing screams as he begged for him to stop.

"AAAAAAARRRRGGGGGGHHHHHHH!!" Davias roared.

"You like that, don't you?" The Hunter teased, flashing his teeth as his victimized sibling sank to his knees. His arm was still hoisted above him, held tight and secure.

"Make. It. STOP!" He demanded.

The Hunter dug in his fingertips, tearing his brother's arm open. White light pierced through his skin and shone around the captive grasp. "You have a name, but with my title comes irrefutable power and an unquenchable satiation for demise. So entertain me, won't you? Mortals don't last under my touch for long, and this is the most fun I can remember having."

"Please, brother. I am begging you to—I—Argh!" Davias choked between each of his breaths until tears carved wet trails across his pale face, and his body thrashed about. He pulled and pulled and tried as desperately as he could to break his brother's steadfast grip, but he felt a weakness eating away at him from the inside, like he was being electrocuted from within his soul.

The Hunter cackled above him wordlessly while he gazed down upon his writhing brother, all the while twirling the fingers in his spare hand. It wasn't until his attention was briefly stolen by the emergence of a purple sphere that Davias was able to wrench his arm free and clamor to safety as the two of them watched the eldest sibling appear unexpectedly before them. Helena's thin figure became more visible as Elias' bubble vanished. She immediately scowled at the Hunter as she strode over to where Davias was huddled and offered him her outstretched hand. Elias lingered behind, observing wordlessly while he passed his oar from hand to hand.

"What are you doing, Hunter? I was enjoying a moment to myself when I was interrupted by Eli telling me that you had *gone rogue*?" She asked almost passively as she helped a very confused Davias back to his feet. When no one said anything, she pressured her younger sibling once more. "I did not ask you to assail poor little Davias, did I? *This* is not what I want, Hunter." She turned to face him as she gave Davias a brushing caress on his cheek with one of her fingers. He looked up at his older sister as she comforted him with a perplexed look plastered upon his porcelain face.

The Hunter recoiled in animalistic fear; his instincts told him to protect himself, and so he threw his arms over his head, and immediately smoke began to quiver off of his blackening skin. He collected himself quickly, looking rather ashamed of his fear, and he stammered as he straightened himself out. "I—I was just thinking. I was just thinking of how we could get the upper hand."

"You? Were just thinking? That's not your job, Hunter. In fact, that isn't even your title. You see, when it comes to you and me, I'm the thinker around here. But *officially* speaking," she spoke mockingly as she turned to the younger of her present brothers, "Davias is our little Thinker in the Family." She paused and snapped her visage back to the Hunter and continued to admonish him. "So either way you end up looking at it, Hunt, you don't get to think for yourself. You don't get to make offers to him. We do not need Davias on our side—there is no place to offer him. There are two thrones—mine and Father's, and neither one of us wish for him to meddle in our affairs. What you have done, my little nuisance of a sibling, is you have shown them our hand. So now I have to change some plans due to your negligence and arrogance."

Davias clutched his scarred arm as he raised his voice to his eldest sister. "What makes you think you're so powerful, Helena? First you send Hunter to be your errand boy, and when he inevitably goes astray like the animal he is, you, in turn, have to leverage our youngest brother to keep him in line. And what promises have you had to make to keep them in your favor? Power? Darkness? Control? I know why you don't want me on your side—because you've realized that those things cannot keep me in line. You would have nothing to lord over me with. You're absolutely powerless against me—and so it is only easier for you to resist me than to accept me. And Madrina, and Eliza. You lack all sense of morality—and apparently, so do these two. Hunter's lack of thought doesn't surprise me, but you, Elias, should be disappointed with how you have aligned yourself. You've the most potential for greatness here, but I promise you: the more you ally yourself with Helena, the more she will hurt you in the end. We will all be tasked with cleaning up whatever mess it is that she creates."

Helena's hair bobbed as she began to laugh loudly in his direction. She thrust a hand behind her to signal Elias to stay in place. Her eyes flashed a bright scarlet in the pale moonlight that highlighted her skin as a smirk stretched across her face and she clapped her two hands together. The entire area plunged into a thick, inky, pool of lightless pitch. At first, the light was immediately blotted out, but soon thereafter, a flood of sticky, invisible tar began to swallow everything around them. Davias watched the ruby-red eyes glare with satisfaction through the blackness as he heard the Hunter transform into a crow and take flight. Elias' purple bubble illuminated and grew to envelope both him and Helena as they disappeared from sight.

Davias began to really struggle against the strong gravitational tides of whatever material Helena had created. His head went under, and he began to choke on a swirling mass of the tar when he managed to reach one hand up and break the surface tension. He tried to shout out loud to Eliza to come and rescue him, but the effort to make sound simply exhausted him even further. Only just as his consciousness began to fade did a warming, pink sphere appear out of nowhere, to pick him up and take him back home to the Pre-Life.

CHAPTER 9

THE ESSENCE

"Father! You'll never believe what just happened!" Helena boasted loudly as she stepped through Elias' portal into an illustrious-looking throne room with ornate, black stone stairs that fanned out the further they went downward. Rolls of red fabric ran the length of the room, giving every surface an undeniable blemish of ruby. Atop the staircase sat a pair of different-but-matching thrones, both created from the bones of a massive, long-extinct beast and painstakingly transported to the After-Life by Helena for the sole purpose of luxurious extravagance.

"My beautiful Helena! Did you get that matter sorted out between your brothers?" Father's voice denoted a hint of glee as he welcomed his daughter back to her throne. As she took her place by his side, Father pivoted in his massive chair and propped himself up on one elbow, so he could sit, stare, and listen with absolute intent.

"My brethren are situated. Hunter was trying to coerce the Thinker into joining our ranks. By the time Elias had gotten us there, we saw Davias down on his knees being tortured by the Hunter's mere touch. A simple touch, Father. From his fingertips and he was in agony. With power like that, I could rule over all of them. Instead of attempting to drown them all in primordial ooze," she fiendishly licked her lips as she replayed the recent events for Father to depict.

Father—either by hubris or by intention—ignored his daughter's obvious greed and envy and instead asked her with wanting malaise, "Where are they now, your brothers?"

"Elias is back on the boat. For now, at least. The Hunter flew off in a panic when I created the tar pit that I hope Davias ended up drowning in. I didn't stick around long enough to witness anything."

Father straightened himself in his throne and leaned forward, this time propping himself on his knee rather than the armrest. "So he escaped?"

"I would hope not," Helena rebutted.

"But you just told me yourself, you didn't bear witness to his demise. So we can only assume he managed to get out. If Hunter flew off, like you said, and this is the Thinker we are talking about, then you most certainly failed in your objective."

"My objective was not to kill Davias, Father—" Helena began, only to be interrupted by her creator.

"Right. Lies have been told here," Father dismissed her arrogantly. Helena rolled her eyes before continuing.

"I just simply wanted to keep everyone in their place. Everyone, from me all the way down the chain to Mother. Everyone except for little Eliza. As far as I see it, if I managed to kill Davias, then Eliza takes his place, and we have the boat to ourselves with Elias. If I didn't drown Davias in tar, then Eliza will have to be the one to rescue him, buying us a little time with the boat to ourselves, allowing Eli to watch without being watched. Either way, I got what I want and Davias got what he deserved."

"You act so recklessly, and yet you have such impressive confidence. With those two traits I would think you'd be a little bit more *successful* with your endeavors. Do you want to know what your problem is, Helena? The one thing I think you lack? Ambition. You waste your talents by lazing away; you waste my efforts by forsaking yourself. Do you ever intend on finishing my bridge? It looks like a pathetic shard of bedrock sticking out of our land. What are you doing about that?" His whiskered face showed signs of exhaustion and annoyance.

"Currently, I'm doing nothing because you're right, Father. I lack ambition, but what I lack even more is motivation, a sense of incentive. You claim that I have gifts, but these gifts are boring without real power. I want what the Hunter has. I want to reign with fear and pain. I want to conquer."

"Maybe this will help," Father said with a solemn seriousness, relinquishing to the wants of his daughter. He reached out with his hand, which seemed to stretch for a mile before him, until his palm swallowed Helena's face, smothering her in his grip. Her body lashed side-to-side while her head stayed in place, and her hands clawed at Father's arm, trying immensely to break free. Grunting, her efforts were quickly wasted. The black aura that hugged Father's body began pulsing as a low, thunderous bass shook their temple. A hum filled the room as the black cloud swelled up like smoke, rising above the two of them until it completely enveloped the surrounding area. It hovered for a moment, circling the air like a swarm of bees until everything stopped simultaneously. Helena stopped thrashing about, the rumbling hum came to a deafening pause, and the black haze came to a halt.

The very next moment, the hum transformed into a loud whooshing of wind as the entire cloud began twisting itself in cords around Father's outstretched hand, like thick black snakes, hurrying themselves to Helena. The blackness stampeded into her eyes, down her throat, and crammed itself into her ears. The entire massive black cloud exhausted itself as it spiraled down

Father's arms to her. She stood still, embraced only by Father's grip, until finally, his fingers let go of her face. Her body fell into a rag doll heap as her back rose and fell in exasperation. Father's throne vanished behind him as he rose to his feet to help her back to her feet.

"What was that?" she managed to ask through her lack of breath.

"That was our next secret weapon. I told you when you were introduced to the After-Life that you were chosen to receive my Essence. You were able to assimilate it all in one attempt. A feat I was not convinced you would be able to accomplish. I thought I would have to go five times, three at best, but it appears you were able to prove me wrong, for once. It appears you were stronger than I thought. And now, indeed, you are stronger than me."

"What does this mean, Father?"

He spoke slowly and deliberately. His words chosen with careful precision. "It means a great deal of things, Helena. First, it means that I can no longer create. I have nothing, no powers, no abilities. Not anymore. I am just another soul, an Immortal, stuck here in the After-Life . . . with you to watch over me for eternity. As of right now, you not only have the *authority* to keep the Hunter and the rest of the Family in line, you have the *capacity* to do so."

Helena looked at her hands in incredulous amazement; her mouth was partially agape. She watched as she twirled her fingers through the air, a snaking trail of thick, black smoke followed her movements.

"Second," Father continued after a moment of silence, "it means you have no equal; you might as well have no rules. As the keeper of Darkness, you have immeasurable powers and capabilities. If you truly wanted, you could rip half of the Universe apart, cascading star systems into black holes just to finish the bridge right here, right now. But as you are now aware of the third change, you have limitless knowledge of the way things are, and the way things can be, and the events that lead to bigger events. Your knowledge now surpasses that of each of your siblings. It might surpass even that of the Thinker. Yes, I kept secrets from you, and yes, I am aware that you have full knowledge of those transgressions now, but none of that matters. With my Essence, you've transcended.

"Fourth, and finally: The Hunter is still vital to our success, for reasons you are now aware of. We need him in order to kill Mother, before she decides to pass her Essence to one of your siblings. If we allow her to succeed at that, then this fight will drag on for more millennia, and the weaponization of our Family will unfortunately continue."

"But you just weaponized me, Father. I am now holding your power, and I can feel it pulse like black lightning through my veins."

"My daughter, you are the Darkness now. Previously, I said that I would, but I did not weaponize you—I transformed you. My fight with Mother has to come to an end. In fact, now it *has* come to an end. Because I know this is the only way to finish it. It is up to you what happens now, and what happens next. I will no longer play any part in the events to come. I will exist among the souls you will reign over."

Father took one of his hands and placed it on Helena's shoulder; his enormous size began to slowly shrink. Helena could feel the absence of energy through his touch. Apprehensively, he patted her shoulder twice before stepping past her, taking his last massive strides down the staircase.

Helena cocked one eye over her shoulder, watching Father march away and out of the temple. Once he was through the marvelous arched gateway, Helena turned around and, with a single clap of her hands, changed the single remaining throne into one with higher regality. One that resonated with elegance, superiority, and grandeur. A second clap of her hands changed the entire tower into a spire that stood as a monument to the Darkness—the stone became denser and darker, shards of jagged slate jutted out at awkward angles.

A third clap of her hands brought down a monstrous lightning strike from the sky, as hundreds of souls were vaporized, their golden dusty entrails swirling their way to Helena's throne. She closed her eyes as her body absorbed the full dose of the golden light. She smiled and sighed in satisfaction as she peeled her eyelids open, uncovering the pools of black that now sat, sunken in her sockets.

"Watcher!" She cried out loudly into the desolate atmosphere of the After-Life. In the reverberation of the following silence, Elias stepped through from the other side of his purple bubble, standing stoically before his sister, who leered down upon him with newfound monstrous authority. "I have to hasten our plans, and you have been so incredibly loyal to me, so I must now reward you. It is almost time for your departure from that boat. Are you ready to start building for me?"

CHAPTER 10

THE BROKEN OAR

"Davias?" a voice bubbled through the ether. And then it faded into a cascade of echoes, falling over one another, as if getting more distant. The silence in between the repetitions eased his consciousness as the sounds stabbed through his nerves. He found himself swimming, sinking in the thick black tar as everything was softly drowned out into nothing.

"Davias?" her voice repeated. Louder. Closer. He felt the soundwaves pull at every thread of his being, drawing him out of the bleakness. Bringing him out of the Darkness. "I'm right here," she whispered. These words did not echo—they hummed, swinging through the air as if lifted on wings instead of singing into the black abyss. He swore he could see the words fluttering above him, trying to pull him out of the ether with their light. It wasn't until they exploded in a shower of blue and red sparks that the blackness broke into brilliance—revealing the familiarly beautiful blue horizon of the Pre-Life to his sight. He gasped for his breath as Mother's warm arms wrapped around him in a welcoming embrace. They sat underneath the Tree of Knowledge, basking in the golden shade provided by the canopy of its many branches and leaves. Davias' eyelids shuddered as he acclimated to the light once again. The last thing he remembered was seeing the Darkness, the feeling of the Darkness—the smell of it, the taste and sound of it as it tried to crush him to death. His every fiber ached with their continued existence.

"I didn't know if I lost you or not," she whispered peacefully, tightening her grip on him. "A little bit of Life brought you back to me. What happened to you?"

"They're out of control, Mother." He gasped, then caught his breath. "The Hunter used Eli to corner me—I'm not even sure where we were; I'm struggling to remember everything he said. He laid his hands on me—Mother, he burned me!" Davias reached out to show Mother the damage his brother had caused. "Then Helena showed up. My head was already spinning from the pain. I think they were trying to recruit me, but then after, she tried to kill me. I think that they were trying to send a message."

"I'm so sorry, Davias. You said you would fight for me, but I never thought it would come to this so quickly. Well, you can consider their message received; I'm assuming you didn't make it to your destination, then? I hope Madrina is fairing okay on her own. I guess our only solace is that all three of them were preoccupied with you; she should be okay. But that would have been the perfect opportunity to get Eliza to the Vessel." Mother drew him closer. They were still underneath the Tree of Knowledge, and she was tracing his hair with her fingers, remembering the first few moments they shared underneath this shade.

"I know my head isn't quite right currently, so forgive me if I ask something I should know, but why do we need to get to this Vessel so urgently, Mother? If Madrina is watching him, and he is safe, then what is our problem?"

"Davias, I used the last of my Essence to bring you back," Mother tried her best to deflect his question, and it worked.

"The last of your—what do you mean, Mother? I thought your

Essence was supposed to be for me?" Davias sat up and turned around to watch Mother's expression as she spoke.

She did not make eye contact, instead her gaze lingered on the golden grass the two of them sat upon as she recalled, "I gave it to Madrina, immediately after you were all created. I needed her to have it, so that she could create the Vessel without Father's knowledge. So that she could create a sanctuary for the three of you. Why else do you think she looks exactly like me? When I imbued her with my Life, I saved a tiny reserve. That reserve was supposed to be for me, to keep me from becoming an Immortal. But that was the price I had to pay to keep from losing another son."

There was a solemn silence as Davias allowed the truth to settle in. As he replayed the words over in his head, a question arose to the surface. "Mother, what is an Immortal?" He stood up and began pacing around while Mother watched him, but never met his eyes.

"Imagine if you had no powers or abilities; you just existed—forever. Everlasting, impermeable, unaffected by Time or the elements, untouched by Life or Darkness. Just *there*. Immortality is the lowest form of existence our Family can take. A Human being that never dies. A wandering soul, lost in search of its peril, but unable to find relief in demise. Few things can put an Immortal in their grave, but the powers of the Hunter, Life, and Darkness. Misused, misaligned, and abused. And I am afraid that is precisely what Helena is beginning to do again."

"You keep speaking nonsensically, Mother. What do you mean by again? Surely this hasn't happened before."

"Things didn't exactly unfold identically to how they are now, but your sister is acting characteristically parallel to how she has done so in the past."

He stopped pacing and confronted Mother as directly as he could. "Then why don't I remember any of this, and when were you going to tell me about your Essence? I am beginning to feel like you have been—and are still—keeping secrets from me. Secrets I should know. I *need* to know everything, Mother. Otherwise you might as well have forsaken me."

She finally relented and met Davias' stare with her own; her fierce, electric blue irises shot right through him as she spoke. "You're right, Davias. I have not been entirely forthright with you, but you must believe me when I tell you these are things that I fully intended on disclosing to you when the moment was absolutely right."

"Well . . ." Davias sighed. He felt deeply disappointed with how Mother had handled this, but that was outside of his control. "Mother, I think that moment might be now."

"I do not disagree with you, but you do not get to call the shots." She stood up to her full height, which had already begun to shrink, and stared down at her son, confused as to how this situation was escalating when she had just saved him from demise.

"Well, I don't think you should be making the calls, now that you're just an Immortal. I have the last of your Life in me, so what are you going to do? Take it back from me?"

"When you know more about what is going on, you can rule over me, Davias, but right now, you still need me for information. If you want answers to your questions, you will uphold your vow of loyalty and continue to fight for me. Fight in my name, because things are only going to get more wicked from here, and you will someday find yourself lost, searching for the will to fight, and you will need to fight for something you believe in when all else seems wrong. So, my son—my *favorite* son—are you with me, or have your siblings actually succeeded in turning you against me?"

"I am with you, Mother. I will always fight for you, in your name. Now, and until the end of Time."

"The Balance is more than just a guideline—it has been the formula to having a successful existence. We have always tried to keep everything in a dichotomized, separate-but-equal harmony. In order to play to that harmony, certain things had to be conducted in secret to prevent any disruptions. To aid in these discretions, Father and I decided it'd be best to remove all of your most core memories between the Iterations to try and avoid repeating any past mistakes. Those of which were mostly on Father and myself, but also the Hunter and your sister, Helena. Every member of the Family shared a little of the blame, but we took care of the faults where they existed, and we tried to pick up from where we left off as best as we could. This transition, and the eradication of your memories came with consequences, but also opportunities. It took more of our energy to orchestrate the necessary changes this time around; we were limited in our aspirations and, thus, our possible outcomes. But what we were limited in we made up for in compromise and novelty—your sisters Madrina and Eliza would come to being through this Reiteration. A desperate attempt to balance the wickedness we saw in Helena and the Hunter. As for my Essence—that was not as planned as everything else was. When Madrina was created, I saw in that very moment, the only opportunity I would get to have any kind of upper hand through our compromises—and I do not regret taking it. Father, and undoubtedly Helena, both must believe you are to inherit that gift, and so with Madrina being the sword-bearer in this war, they should be caught off guard. She has been communing with me in secret—building not just a sanctuary for our Vessel but a haven for whenever we need to use it. An escape route, plotted and coursed just for you. For when the time comes, we may need to act and act fast. The urgency behind all of this, Davias, is to get you and your sister Eliza to touch the Vessel. As simple as that. No tricks or gimmicks. Once you make that contact, you will be granted asylum into that soul, but only after that contact is made. If Helena, or any of the other siblings, beat us to that moment, then they can simply steal the Vessel from us by inhabiting it. They would just need to get into the River Styx. That is why we cannot afford to relinquish our positions here or on the water. We are the last line of defense for whenever that bridge is finished. So I feel the time has come; it is now or never. Let us call Eliza and get you to the Vessel."

"You mean now?"

"Yes, Davias, I mean now. Time is not on our side, remember," Mother indicated to the bridge. "Helena marches closer with each passing moment. Eliza, I need you here, now!" Mother threw her head up and tossed her hands upwards towards the sky as she cried out desperately.

With a burst of magenta, Eliza appeared on the spot. The top of her oar was split off, frayed, and splintered, and her left arm bore burn marks and scars from her shoulder down to her wrist; her clothes were torn in some places and she was wet from head to toe.

She puffed up her chest, trying to catch her breath. "Eli left and the Hunter is on the River! He attacked me, grabbed me, and I couldn't fathom the pain. He made for the oar, and that's when I tried to defend myself. I ran away, and I waited in the Void until you called for me." Eliza stumbled in her pain and caught herself by using a broken oar to prop her limp body up.

Davias stood up, and examined his sister's arm, helping her to stand in the process. In an act of unity, he stretched his own arm out, revealing his identical scars to her. He locked his eyes with hers and nodded silently. "He did the same to me. Do you think you are going to be okay?"

"I'm fine, I think. Eli and I were gathering souls from Life when he just appeared on the gondola behind us," Eliza began. "He was going off crazy about how Helena had given him power now, and he needed the boat. He tried to get my oar, but he didn't succeed." She feebly indicated to the oar she was using as a crutch.

"That means that Helena has his Essence now. She's used Father's powers to strengthen the Hunter," Mother admitted.

She shook her wet, raggedy hair trying to get the drops of water out of it. "He kicked me off the boat and into the water. I was about to go to Madrina until you called me here."

"That's a good idea, Eliza. If Helena has Father's Essence, the two of you need to get to Madrina and the Vessel now, quickly. You both need to touch the Vessel as soon as you can, then get back here. You two will need to jump into the water from the bank of the Pre-Life, that will get you into the Vessel, and from there, you will be gone, hidden and protected from the rest of the Family in Oklahoma. Madrina can find you, but she will need to stay and fight, and she can get herself back to me on her own with my Essence now, but I need to worry about protecting the two of you, so you must hurry, before Helena gets here. Go! NOW!"

Davias looked towards Mother fearfully, still holding his sister's hand for both of their support. He began to feel waves of emotions flowing through him that he had never experienced before—dread, cold, gut-wrenching fear, hollowing him out. For the very first time, a single tear welled up in the corner of Davias' eye as Mother looked at him, smiling weakly as if her optimism had finally wavered. In the same moment, a bright pink light took over his field of view, and the rushing of the river swam past them.

Then, they were back in California in the middle of a midnight storm.

CHAPTER 11

THE ANCIENT SOULS

Using the Darkness as her own personal guide, Helena tried to sense her brother's whereabouts in the fabric of reality. She had finally given Elias another chance to free himself from being confined to the River Styx. The Hunter was about to take his place and oar while the Watcher travelled to Life. Fascinated by the power imbued within the oar he held in his hands, the Hunter leered over the edge and spied on his siblings. Eliza and Davias cowered with Mother in the After-Life. Madrina stood in the cold California rain. Elias was using the Darkness that he had been gifted to create Helena's city. He looked for him, but Father was unable to be found.

Helena stood at the threshold of the magnificent gateway that adorned the entrance to the temple which swallowed the entirety of the skyline that was once the After-Life. The outside of the temple angled upwards with steep slopes of blackened slate. The slates created sharp spikes that reached as high as they could, like long, fierce stalagmites. The sloping angles surrounded a lone, stone tower whose smoothness made it stand out among the rest of the black rock. At the top of the tower was an overlook that offered a view of the black bridge stretching through the Void of

Impossible Things. A black mist swirled around Helena in thick, dark particles that resembled gnats, clinging to her presence. Beneath her, at the base of the temple, an army of a million souls stood at the ready. Their colors ranged from a sickly, miserable grey to a shade darker than the blackest of pitch. They did not move, they did not flinch, they did not flutter; they stood at the ready, waiting for their command to march forward towards the mouth of the bridge that sat, just as ready as the souls—black, still, and cold. Helena called to the Hunter, beckoning him to join her.

An audible pop reverberated in the overlook from behind Helena, who was perched close to the edge, assembling massive blocks onto the bridge's construction. An acid-green cloud dissolved into mist on the floor as the Hunter appeared in a crouched position, bracing himself with one hand on the ground and the other clutching Eli's oar. He straightened himself up, brushing off what little dust gathered on him as he approached his sister.

"I really like these oars. I've always wanted to travel on my own," the Hunter said in admiration. "Where is Father?"

"He's around; I have something to show you," Helena said, moving another piece of slate into place with her hands. The rocks were so far away; they were almost minuscule as they floated on the horizon. At the end of the bridge, the Void of Impossible Things stood infinitely large and immaculately white, except for the gaping wound where the bridge had pierced right through it. "His mistake was giving me the ability to create all that I wanted."

"Why was that?" Hunter asked flatly while he peered out over the edge of the temple's overlook.

"As an engine to his plot, it was all he could do to succeed. However, Father is a fool, and ultimately he miscalculated."

"Miscalculated what?" the Hunter clarified, his tone was just as flat as before.

"My absolute power, little brother, I am now the most power-ful out of all of our little Family. Even Davias with Mother's pathetic Essence couldn't catch up to my level. Victory is at hand; I just need to close my fingers."

Hunter's tone broke; his pitch reflected an eagerness. "I assume I have a part to play in this. What do you need me to do for you?"

"Hunter," Helena clicked her tongue. "Certainly by now you've realized that you've been playing your part. It is because of you that we have a million-soul army at our disposal."

"You told me you had something to show me?" The Hunter turned back to look at his sister.

"Oh, speaking of our army, I most certainly do," Helena outstretched her fist to him and uncurled her fingers into a beckoning open palm. "Take my hand and come with me."

The Hunter dutifully placed his hand in hers, and as immediately as she clasped his, the two of them began to sink down through the stone floor, far, far below them. They came to the middle of a large open room with two gigantic cages in the center of the area. Around the walls were cells as large as boats, secured with thick, perpendicular black bars. From inside these cells came growling, screeching, and roaring sounds, the likes of which the Hunter could never imagine. Massive pairs of red-colored eyes peered at him through the abyss. He tentatively walked towards one of the cells as a giant tentacle rapidly unfurled through the bars, coiling around his leg tightly. It began pulling him in closer with enough strength that he was useless to resist it.

"Kraken, release my little brother," Helena commanded coolly, waltzing up beside her sibling, who was visibly shaken after regaining his balance as the tentacle released its grasp, snaking back between the bars.

"What . . . are these?" The Hunter asked in disbelief, staring through the bars with a mixed look of anger and confusion.

"These are the most Ancient Souls that Father and Mother decided to keep after the Iteration. I don't think they could actually get rid of them without disturbing the Balance. I found them, locked away far below and have decided to bring them to the surface. Once the bridge is complete and our army marches through the Void, our beasts will follow, and we will submit the rest of them to damnation."

"You can control these monstrosities?" he raised his voice over a deafening roar.

"With the Darkness, not only can I control them, I can *destroy* them if I wanted to. Once we have access to the Pre-Life, these beasts will carve through our siblings, and then I can bring these creatures back to Life myself, and we can begin harvesting souls and growing our army expeditiously. Something that I wish Mother could watch, but she won't be around long enough to witness my domination over her precious Humans. And right now, Elias is creating my empire in Life. A refuge for you and me, a palace bathed in Darkness and dominion, swarming with lowlifes and miscreants."

Her brother strode between the cages, stopping to gaze inside each one. Some of the cells were too dark to see into, but the creatures that he could see terrified him; beasts that he had never seen in creation before, monsters with horns and massive heads, disproportionate bodies and eyes that pieced with menacing malevolence. But there was one cell, in the far corner that captured his attention. It was eerily quiet, unlike the rest, and stood cold and still as if unoccupied. When the Hunter got closer, he could see faintly into the confines: the shrunken, bearded figure of Father was chained and shackled to the wall, his head hung heavily against his chest.

"Father?" Hunter gently whispered, afraid of what might be true.
"Hunter? Is that you?"
"W-what happened?"

"Helena did. She locked me in here." He could only manage a faint whisper. Father's voice was just as weak as his body.

"I thought we were getting ready to fight?" His son asked him dejectedly. Helena quietly approached from behind, placing her arm over her sibling's shoulder as she did so. She pulled him close, so that their heads were almost touching.

"And we are, brother. Relinquishing the Darkness weakened him more than we thought it would, so I am just ensuring that Father is safely in place for our big finale. After millennia, all of his planning and hard work shouldn't go to waste, should it? All I am doing is making sure that Father witnesses what he has yearned to see for too long."

"But—" Hunter began. He forced himself to stop talking.

"But what, little brother? Are you concerned?" Helena snapped aggressively, staring straight past him, into the cell at Father's figure.

The Hunter hesitated to respond. He mulled over the possibility that he was concerned, and what that might mean of Helena's perception of his worthiness to ascend in his power. "What if I was concerned, Helena?" he confessed, timidly.

"You shouldn't be; you've been loyal to him from the start. You've always served him well. More to the point, you've been incredibly loyal to me, brother, and have served me better than I could have anticipated, better than Eli. And so for that, I will ensure that you are rewarded, when the time comes."

"Rewarded with what?"

"Well, if we eliminate Mother, I will need someone here to tend to the After-Life and the Pre-Life as I take what will rightfully be mine: a throne amongst the Humans in Life."

"What about Father? He has always existed in the After-Life. Why not let him continue watching over?"

Helena replied with the same aggressive assertion she did prior, but this time, she turned her gaze to stare coldly at her sibling instead. "Father is without Essence; he has parted with his energies. He is an empty shell, a reflection and culmination of his former efforts. He could not manage, and I have no intent of giving his Essence back, so I will ask you again, will you take my place in the After-Life when our fight is over?"

He mulled this over in his head, the thoughts flipped and tumbled over each other as he scrambled to produce a response. Slowly, after a moment, he turned his head to the right to face Helena, who was already waiting to look her brother in the eye. He managed a single nod in affirmation as Helena's smile slowly crept across her jaw once more.

"Everything that transpires beyond this moment is going to be *immensely* satisfying for me. So I hope you are truly prepared, Hunter." Helena walked up to the bars and draped her arms inside the cell as she peered through the dark, her deep black eyes locked on Father's withering, giant figure. There was an extensive silence as she thought to herself while peering at her captive creator. "Hunter! I've had an idea!" she said without turning back around. "What do you think about running one last errand for me? If I give you a gift to keep, do you think you could get something done for me with it?" She snapped her fingers, and a wisp of smoke appeared and snaked around the air menacingly. She whispered into the Darkness, "Elias, I'll need you too."

"What kind of a gift did you have in mind?" he greedily replied. With a slight chuckle, Helena turned around as Elias appeared silently in the background and waited. She began slowly walking towards the Hunter. The skin on both of their arms immediately turned black as night as Helena's eyes grew red once more, like embers, just for the briefest of moments before cooling down back into black hunks of coal.

"I'll give your current powers a significant enhancement. You are the Hunter, capable of reaping and killing any Human. Except for one—Mother's little Vessel. What if I removed that limitation? What if I gave you more than enough power to reap that child? If you do that for us, I will release Father from his shackles, just for you."

He nervously glanced towards Father, with his head hung low, then turned back towards Helena, "If you promise to keep your word, I will go ahead and do that." She turned away from the bars, and this time, she locked her eyes with her brother's emerald irises.

"*You* do not get to hide behind ultimatums; I already gave you my word, I want you to give me yours. Now," Helena leaned in closer to her brother, who stood still as a statue, locked solid in fear as she slowly circled and coiled around him like a snake. His hand tightened his grip on the wooden paddle in apprehension.

Through gritted teeth, Hunter succumbed to the pressure of his decision. "You have my word, Helena, that I will reap the Vessel and hand deliver the soul to you in exchange for Father's freedom."

"Excellent, brother, you chose your loyalties wisely. Grab ahold of my wrists, and do not let go."

He reluctantly placed the oar on the ground and took his hands and re-positioned them so that he could grasp his sister's wrists, as instructed. In return, Helena did the same, grabbing onto his arms. Gradually, the blackness on their skins grew in intensity as it began to crackle and smolder. An intensity welled between the two of them as waves of gravity poured through their beings. He could feel his fingertips turn to ice as gentle whisps of smoke escaped his skin through small, burning cracks. The two of them released their grip, and he began to continually turn his hands over and over, marveling as they crackled with cold, black flames.

"Your siblings will be waiting close by when you arrive; I sense that Mother has already sent them to complete the process. I have faith that you will get this done for me, and once you do, I want you to return to my side and from there, we will march across to the Pre-Life. Hunter, you'll take your brother's spot on the raft, while Eli, you finish building, and then both of you get to the Vessel. Quickly, then we can move on with our final agenda," she spoke in Eli's direction, nodding as she did so. Eli responded without even so much as an acknowledgment as he held out his hand towards his brother. The Hunter plucked the oar off the ground and extended it gruffly. Once he grabbed hold, the two of them were swallowed by lavender, as they were transported to the boat.

. . .

Alone, Eliza stood watch on the ferry, paddling from one invisible shore to another, gathering handfuls of souls ready to return to their unknown home. The unseen waters of the River Styx wound through all of existence, the current always ebbing and flowing to guide the Watchers where they were needed—even if the craft were to be unguided by anyone in the Family, it would still flow along in the stream as departed souls embarked on their celestial cruise.

"Where are you, Eli?" disappointed in her twin brother, she sighed. She looked downwards into the water and conjured an image of him with the Hunter and Helena. He stood silently, but Eliza could just barely hear Helena and the Hunter having a discussion—she couldn't make out any words, but she watched Elias stand by as Helena transferred an enormous amount of energy into the Hunter. His hands ignited in Darkness, and then she watched as he picked up the oar and handed it to Elias. The very next moment, Eliza felt the stability of the boat change as the two of them materialized behind her. She quickly straightened up and tried not to make it seem too obvious that she had been spying on them.

"Liza," her twin greeted her. "I'm leaving the boat again for a little. Hunter is taking my place this time so you aren't alone. If you need help, ask for it. Please be safe; I'll be back soon." He handed his oar back to the Hunter, who greedily snatched it between both of his hands. His eyes stared at the ancient grains of wood with maddening hunger locked away in his irises. "Hunter, let Eliza take the lead on this. It's boring, but it's simple work. Don't mess this up, please." With an exchanged look between his brother, Elias departed in his glass dome, leaving the two of them alone.

Eliza kept her oar in the water. She shifted her weight as she felt the distrust settle into her nerves. She tried keeping her attention focused on Hunter and the souls in the middle of the boat. Her brother was completely infatuated with Eli's oar. He continued to marvel at it while he gently ran his hands down the rough material. Then, without any warning, he spoke. "I know you're watching me. Watcher."

"That's what I do, Hunter," she replied as cordially as she could, though the slightest hint of annoyance mixed with fear underscored her words. "I watch."

"Have you been watching me a lot?" he teased, placing the handle of the oar on the gondola and leaning the paddle towards his younger sister. "Do you *like* watching me?"

"Just because I have to, doesn't mean that I enjoy watching anyone. I don't. I really don't like doing it."

"That's a shame; Eli likes watching. He's great at it, might even be better than you, since you don't seem to appreciate your gift."

"Do you like . . .what you do?" she asked curiously while still keeping him just inside of her peripheral view. The Hunter lost all poise and pompousness in his surprise at this question.

"Are you kidding?" he scoffed. Cradling the oar close to his bare chest, he confessed, "I love it; I can't get enough of it. And with this oar, I can feel the possibilities in my hands. I could travel anywhere, reap anyone in an instant. You're an idiot if you don't like what you've been gifted with. I'd give anything to keep one of these."

"Well you can't keep it, it's Eli's," Eliza stopped him quickly. She finally turned to face him, all while keeping one hand on her own oar that was still submerged in the clear water.

"I don't think he'd mind if I kept it. He can get around just fine without it, after all. I'm the one that really needs one of these. Trying to reap Humans is draining if I have to put any effort into it. And being a damn crow isn't helpful either."

"He won't let you borrow it either, Hunter. You don't get one of these. We do. You have your gifts, we have ours. That's the way it is, and that's the way it's supposed to stay. Don't you care about the Balance at all?"

"Not one iota, little sis. You really don't think he'll let me keep it?" He looked downward, towards the handle resting at the base of the craft they floated upon.

"No, he needs it." She pulled her oar out of the water and pinned it against her body as she placed her hands on her hips defiantly.

"Then why don't I just take yours?" The Hunter lunged forward, dropping Eli's oar with a clatter as the souls scrambled towards the opposite side of the gondola in fright.

His hands clutched both the oar he sought and his sister's arm in the crossfire. He cackled with maniacal insanity as they wrestled for Eliza's oar. Her skin began to blister and boil everywhere he touched her arm, and the longer he held, the worse it grew. She barely managed a grip on the paddle as she felt her flesh begin to melt and char down to her bones.

She wanted to scream. She tried to scream, but the combination of the pain her brother was inflicting and the amount of effort it took to keep a hold on the ancient paddle robbed her of any wind she held in her chest. Every fiber of her body began to grow white-hot as she felt the black flames lick at her Essence.

The wood began to smolder and splitter from the struggle between the two of them.

"Stop. Resisting. You're going to break it," the Hunter managed through snared teeth; his greasy hair flailed side to side, and his acid-green eyes flared with fury. He finally let go of her skin and placed both hands on the weakening handle.

Immediately relieved from the searing pain, Eliza placed one of her bare feet on her brother's exposed chest and kicked backwards with full force. The oar snapped in two—scattering shimming splinters soaring across the craft. Both siblings fell backwards. The Hunter landed forcefully on his back. Elias reappeared behind his twin and caught her before she fell. The souls swarmed to cower behind Eli as he helped Eliza to her feet and shuffled himself in front to protect her.

He slowly walked over and placed the heel of his foot square in the middle of the Hunter's sternum before he could get up. He knelt down, low enough that their noses started to touch, and he whispered to his brother very angrily.

"Stay down, you animal! I knew you couldn't be trusted."

"You're back," Hunter stated the obvious. He made a move to grab Eli's ankle with his burning hands. Eli straightened up, moving his foot out of the way before bringing it back down with a rib-snapping stomp.

His older brother choked. Then laughed. "Did you finish building your little city?" Hunter teased. Then another stomp. Eliza heard the wooden boards of the gondola groan under the pressure.

"You'll keep your hands off of her, and me." Elias turned towards his twin. "Eliza, go. Hide in the Void—you'll be safer there. I'll come get you when it's clear." She nodded and held onto the broken handle as she left in her magenta bubble without saying another word.

Elias took his foot off of his brother's chest and turned around to retrieve his oar. He stood guard in front of the crowd of cowering souls, holding the paddle defensively as he waited for his brother to stand back on his feet. Doubling over from the crushing that his torso had withstood, the Hunter barely had a chance to speak before Eli grabbed him by his vest and pulled him in close.

"You are no longer welcome aboard. From now on, you must find your own way to get around. I'm *DONE* with you!" he shoved his brother backwards towards the edge of the craft and swung at him with the oar. As the wood connected, his brother disappeared with a burst of bright green smoke.

Eli dematerialized into the Void to search for his sister, but found no sign of her. "Eliza!" he cried out with one hand cupped around his mouth, the other clutching his paddle.

"Eliza!" his echo screamed back at him. Dejected, he rematerialized onto the boat and continued forward, looking at the uneasy group of souls left in his care.

"Don't worry everyone, I will protect you," he managed to speak softly and coolly as he placed the paddle in the water and began rowing once more.

. . .

The Hunter materialized on his back on the ground next to an isolated access road. A soft rainfall fell from the darkened night sky, dampening the concrete and matting his hair. He opened his eyes and blinked upward, clutching his chest in pain. The side of his face oozed a black blood from where he had been struck by his brother.

He sat up and scrambled to his feet as lightning flashed in the distance, lighting up the dusty sky in a maroon and brown spectacle. A gust of wind picked up as the lone sibling stretched his arms out wide, his blackened fingers casting off smoky strings in the rain as his skin rippled and converted into rough feathers.

His body shrunk rapidly as his face contorted, and he took to his crow form and soared into the skies, circling overhead.

He swooped and dove through different neighborhoods, coasting on the wind behind him. His eyes were tuned into the Darkness, looking for any sign of his siblings. His feathers wicked away the rain as it splattered on his crown and wings. Faintly, in the distance, he recognized the house, a two-story structure decorated with a brick chimney, a large covered patio, and a sizable pool in the backyard. In the front of the house, a winding walkway sat soaked from the rain, a series of small rocks lined the sides. On one of these rocks, he saw Madrina sitting in perfect posture, looking towards the shelter attentively; her royal blue outline illuminated the raindrops as they fell around her.

He flew down to the backyard underneath the covered patio. As he came down to land, he transformed back into his regular Human-like appearance. He straightened out his vest and approached the wall of the house. He placed his palm on the handle, and the door almost seemed to swing itself open, inviting him inside.

He wandered through the halls of the house, welcoming himself to stop, and for the very first time, he admired how the mortals lived. Four beautiful faces smiled back at him in a photograph hanging on the wall. A mother and father and their two boys, one of which the Hunter immediately recognized as the Vessel. The other child had a sense of familiarity, too, that the Hunter couldn't quite place. He continued to slowly walk through the house in the dark until he came to a hallway that ended with three closed doors, one in front of him and one on both of his sides. He stopped, not knowing which door to choose.

In his hesitation, he heard a trio of his siblings' familiar voices. He grabbed for the closest door handle to his right and swung inside without a sound, quietly latching it shut. In the dark, he quickly examined the room in eager anticipation. The moment was upon him. He was almost to the bed when he heard a gentle footfall on the other side. He rushed up and pressed his ear to the door, listening attentively as he smeared his black blood on the frame. He waited until his siblings had passed. When he turned back around, the child was sitting upright in the bed, staring straight at him.

"Who are you?" his innocent voice whispered over the muffled raindrops in the moonlight.

Startled, Hunter pointed at his chest. "You can see me?" he asked. The child nodded wordlessly, pulling the blankets up to cover half of his face.

"Are you a monster?" his quivering voice asked from behind the comforter.

"No one has ever been able to see me before. Are you the Vessel?" the Hunter got to his knees and shuffled across the carpeted floor to get a closer look.

The kid didn't move or say anything at first. Then, his head slowly began to move up and down in a nod. "I know who you are, Mathias." Hearing his *name* shook the Hunter to the core of his Essence. He felt his skin grow cold, and his vision narrowed as he panicked.

"You *are* the Vessel," he breathed in disbelief. He placed a single hand on the child's arm. He could feel the soul detach from the body, and he immediately fell limp and tumbled out of the bed.

His success felt less than satisfactory. It almost saddened him that Mother would involve such an innocent, vulnerable child in the Family's affairs. Almost. Then he shook his head, trying to abandon all feelings of sympathy as he hiked to his feet and stomped to the bedroom door. He wrenched it open and followed the hushed voices of his siblings across the hall. When he opened the door that concealed them, he realized immediately that he hadn't, in fact, been successful. He had failed. He felt his chest sink—panic sunk in as he began to feel desperation and sympathy seep into his fibers—and the next thing he knew he was crashing into the floor.

Madrina tackled him and held him pinned down before he had a chance to make any other movements. He ignored everything she was saying to him as he helplessly watched Eliza and Davias complete their ritual with the Vessel.

CHAPTER 12

THE ELEVENTH HOUR

Madrina long awaited alone near the edge of a quaint neighborhood road. The sidewalk glistened with a mixture of freshly fallen rain and a soft reflection of the moon's persistent glow. Outlines of humble rainclouds haunted the sky. Madrina's skin and silk robes remained dry through the onslaught of droplets, and her hair still hung in pristine strands. She watched as the moonlit-dappled figures of her brother and sister approached through a glass dome.

"We need to hurry. Someone is coming," Madrina stated to her arriving siblings indirectly. She displayed no urgency. Her gaze was fixed upon the home's front door. It was a faded blue and illuminated by a single light in the alcove with a handful of potted plants that decorated the doorstep where a welcome mat was currently being waterlogged by the downpour of rain.

"The Hunter," Davias said punctually. "I can sense him. It goes in and out, but I can feel him. Somewhere above us."

Next to her stood Davias and Eliza, having just transported themselves to the adjacent walkway. "What should we do if he sees us?" Eliza worried, leaning on the shortened oar she carried. Though the rain was pelting their heads, Madrina's Essence allowed the three of them to remain dry, like they were wrapped in an invisible blanket.

Madrina explained, "If he sees us, he sees us, sister. By now, everyone knows what we are doing. If we're lucky, we can stop him from getting to the Vessel. Once we are inside the shelter, we can find our Vessel and make contact. That's it—then you need to carry all of us out and back to Mother. As long as we do this quickly, there won't be any room for interference from our brother. Stick close to me if you are afraid," as she reassured plainly, the pitter-patter of rainfall added a cadence behind her words. There was a brief silence filled only with the sounds of the rain.

"Hey you two, I can't sense him anymore, but he's closing in," Davias warned his sisters with a hushed whisper that was acknowledged by a pair of nods.

Eliza spoke a little louder. Her squeaky voice was staccatoed by the worry in her chest. "Do you think Mother's plan will work? What will happen if he does catch us?"

"There are many parts of Mother's plan, but I have faith that the parts that need to go our way, will. Like I said, Eliza, I will be able to protect you from the Hunter if that is what you are truly worried about. Davias can try to give us another warning if he is able." It wasn't a question. Madrina turned to him, and he nodded in unity.

"He attacked me," Eliza held up her oar to indicate the fallout. "On the boat, he ambushed me, and the oar broke when I tried to protect myself."

"I'm so sorry, little sister. Here, give that to me. These have been around for a very long time. They hold an incredible amount of power and need to be cared for. Please, let me see if I can do something about this for you." Madrina extended her arm and took the handle of the oar from her sister, and as she held it in her hands, the brown wooden grains and crevices glowed in a bright, electric blue hue. The wood let out a painful, complaining creak as the paddle grew back, like a limb regenerating. The bright blue light faded, revealing a new, polished white sheen to the wood, almost like a pearl. Eliza gasped in excitement as she snatched it back from Madrina, who relinquished it compassionately, giving her sister a gentle smile in the process. Eliza squealed with glee, as her worry washed away in the rain.

"Madrina?" Davias modestly spoke up.

"Is something troubling you too, brother? Speak your mind. Do it quickly so we can move on with it."

"Can you explain to me how this is all supposed to work? I mean, what good is the Vessel going to do us if Mother isn't going to fight and Helena has Father's Essence?"

"Just because Mother isn't *going* to fight doesn't mean that she isn't *actually* fighting. She's in this just as much as the rest of us are."

"But . . ." he paused, considering whether he should say the words trying so desperately to escape. Madrina gave him an expression that encouraged him to finish the sentence. "She gave you her Essence." He sounded defeated.

"Yes, she did. Is that what's upsetting you?"

With no consideration this time, Davias just went ahead and said what was on his mind. "I thought I was supposed to inherit it," his muscles tightened, anticipating what Madrina would say next. "I thought that was my destiny."

"Destiny or not, you don't need to feel jealous, Davias. Yes, that was the original intention—for you to receive her Essence. You see, if you believed you were supposed to receive her Essence, then Father and Helena were going to believe that, too. If there is anything I have learned from convening with Mother's memories is that, sometimes, tactfully speaking, there is more value to deception than honesty. Alone, the truth is just a series of facts represented plainly that anybody can take advantage of. But deception is a series of valuable facts often cloaked by one simple misdirection. Mother explained the Balance to you? Think of it like that. Truth adds value to the lies; lies add value to the truth. If no one ever lied to you, everything would always be taken at face value. Mother's intent was to catch Helena and Father off guard with the truth. She is fighting with us, Davias. She's playing a mental game. Father's ultimate intention was just to deceive from the start, which forced him to reveal the truth before too long. Deception and misdirection are not always bad, brother; they just don't feel good when you have the moral high ground to begin with. I'm sorry if you feel tricked." Davias nodded quietly and slowly, trying to understand what she was saying to him.

"Here in Life, Davias, Time moves differently than in our Realm. You know that Time flows from the Void of Impossible Things—like blood from a wound. The Void is the wound in the Universe from Mother and Father's previous transgressions. Time doesn't touch our Realm because it is the scab that formed from the wound—the After-Life and the Pre-Life stay untouched because Time flows downward, not outward. It can only flow one way, and the victims of that cascade reside down below. Here, in Life," Madrina explained as lightning flashed overhead, brightening up the sky with a dim light show.

"Why are you telling me this?" Davias asked innocently.

"I have to emphasize the importance of this mission, for Mother's sake. Do you know why you have to touch the Vessel? Why we all need to touch the Vessel?"

"Probably not as well as you do," Davias remarked, then added, "he's closer, I can feel him again. He seems lost."

Madrina ignored his tongue-in-cheek remark, dropped her helpful demeanor, and let her pride carry her on. "There are several reasons we are here. First of which, we need a strong contingency in case we are wrong about Father and Helena's intentions—but that seems unlikely as currently there is a massive bridge looming on the horizon in the Pre-Life. The second reason, that very bridge has torn a hole through the fabric of the Void of Impossible Things. The more we create wounds in the fabric of existence, the more we risk losing absolutely everything. *Everything*," she emphasized. "She has the power to annihilate inorganic matter and rematerialize it elsewhere. That process punches tiny holes in the weave of the Universe, which spells trouble if she decides to start ripping holes in the Void like it's nothing. Time will spill out in our Realm and everything that is ours will be irreversibly contaminated, and eventually, everything will fall apart because Time is unavoidably and irrevocably toxic. So, the third reason you, me, and Eliza are here: The Vessel affords us an anonymous hiding place. You cannot hunt what you cannot find, and Helena can only get stronger by hunting us and assimilating us and our powers. So by removing some of us from play, we can take away any advantage that she could possibly gain. Otherwise, she could cast all of us out of the After-Life and Pre-Life and hunt us down with an unmatched ferocity. That would be a fight we could never win. The fourth and final reason we need the Vessel is because we have already invested so many resources into this, that we'd be subjecting ourselves to sabotage if we were to abandon it now."

"What good will hiding do for us? It is an admission of defeat, is it not?" Davias challenged.

"Not exactly. Think about it for a moment. When Darkness and Life fought all of those ages ago, Life was able to hide from the Darkness for a while, and the fighting ceased. Like I said, you cannot fight what you cannot find. During that time, Darkness grew weaker because he used his energy to try to sustain his growth. Helena may have Darkness in her now, but she is not in the Darkness—she can never be. She, like the rest of us created in the Void, was born with Time in her veins, so her powers, like the rest of ours, will drain and diminish, whereas I have Life in me, and I am in Life—I have been for quite a while. What Mother never told you, Davias, is that she has once again found a clever way of reuniting her Essence with her true body: this planet. I have been assimilating unpredictable amounts of energy. My powers are growing, perhaps stronger than Helena's could ever be. The Hunter may be able to hurt you two, but not me. In fact," Madrina paused as she extended one arm to both of her siblings, taking their scarred hands in her own. She stated with a pronunciation of heroism in her voice, "I can undo his damage."

The burns and scars on both of their arms began to fade as the skin smoothed itself out, whimsically returning to normal. "Like I said," she continued. "Mother's plan has many facets to it, and I have overseen each and every detail since the beginning." She stopped talking abruptly. Davias held up a hand and placed a finger over his lips to hush his sister.

"He's almost here; we need to go inside now," his words were barely audible.

A look of panic flushed across Eliza's face as Madrina ushered the three of them together. "Eliza, take us inside. I won't let him hurt you. Keep your oar close to you and make sure he does not grab on so we can get a clear shot out of there once we are done. Let's move."

Eliza held out her oar, and both her sister and brother placed a single hand on the newly regenerated, polished white wood. They disappeared without another sound and rematerialized inside the front door. They crept through the house, taking extra precautions to create the lightest footfall as possible. Madrina halted at the end of a hallway and whispered so quietly they had to strain to hear her. "His room is on the left at the end of the hallway; you two just need to make contact, long enough for your Essence to make contact with his soul. After that, Eliza, you need to get us out of here and take us back to Mother."

"Has Eli touched the Vessel yet? I've been too distracted," Eliza remarked, the trademark note of worry still in her voice.

"For once, I was the Watcher. He was just here, actually. I'm not sure why, but I'd assume he got it done before leaving. Which reminds me, when you are in the Vessel, he will be drawn to a beacon. There's a town I created called Crooks. It's obscured from most of history."

"How come Mother never explained any of this to me? Why am I only just now hearing this from you?" Davias whispered as they turned down the hallway leading away from the kitchen.

"I'll say it again, brother," Madrina began as they slowly drew nearer to the door. "Mother's plan had many facets, keeping you in the dark was unfortunately one of them. It is not my fault." Madrina defended and placed her hand on the doorknob, and it too gracefully pushed forward, revealing a room that was very dimly lit by the moonlight that trickled through baby-blue curtains that were hastily splayed across the window. The room was tidy, but small. Pictures adorned the wall, and a single pair of shoes sat next to a pile of discarded clothes next to a bed where a small body lay comfortably resting.

"Davias, you can go first." With that, he stepped forward and gently curled his hand on the boy's forehead. Almost instantly, the body glowed with a dim orange light until Davias removed his hand and took a step back. "Eliza, stay ready. You'll need to teleport us out of here soon."

Davias walked backwards and rejoined the other two close to the doorway. As he returned, his peripheral vision noticed the door swinging open to the side. He pointed in shock, and his sisters turned around swiftly, coming face to face with the Hunter whose grimacing green eyes pierced through the darkness, lit with a ravenous hunger that screamed malevolence.

"Eliza, go now! Do it quickly!" Madrina half whispered, half shouted as she tackled the Hunter. Scrambling, Eliza trampled to the bed frame, hastily slapping her hand across the kid's forehead as his body flashed a subtle magenta color after a few seconds. She went to turn back around but stumbled over her feet which caused her to drop the oar to the floor with a solid thud. The Hunter's eyes followed the falling oar, and he tried to advance forward. Madrina raised one arm straight out and braced it against the center of his chest, holding him back.

"Hello, Madrina, it's been a long while, hasn't it? You wouldn't happen to know where I can find our littlest sister? She and I weren't finished with something!" He cackled through the blackness that was beginning to run down his face. He took both of his blackened, smoking hands and gripped Madrina's arm. At the same time, Madrina's forearm started glowing a violent cobalt blue as a force wave propelled the Hunter backwards and out onto the hallway floor.

"Eliza, get up!" Davias cried as he scurried to his sister. He grabbed the oar and her arm while pulling her to her feet. "We need to go!"

"Wait, you two," Madrina suddenly changed her mind. "We have to take him with us," Madrina stopped them before they could retreat. Both of them responded by giving identically confused looks.

"Why? We don't need him. We need to get back to Mother," Davias urged.

"The Hunter—he's stronger now. His hands had more energy pulsing through them than I ever remember feeling from him before. I promise you, our brother can kill him now. I can't stop him, so we have to take him with us so he can't come back here," Madrina looked between Eliza and Davias as she explained this, then the three of them looked towards the Hunter as he struggled to find his footing again. His bare chest bore a smoldering blue hole the size of a fist that tunneled straight through his body, allowing his siblings to see the hallway on the other side of his torso. Black liquid dripped from the sinewy wound before it slowly began to fuse back together.

Madrina walked over and took a hold of him by his greasy, black hair, wrenching him in close to her, and she walked to the other two and placed her hand on Eliza's oar as Davias did the same. Eliza tapped the bottom of the oar on the floor as a pink bubble inflated around the four of them. The familiar rushing water sound echoed loudly in the bubble as the black opaqueness around them dissipated into the Pre-Life.

CHAPTER 13

THE BRIDGE

There was a looped walkway at the peak of the tower that Helena had erected which served as an overlook to all of the After-Life and the souls that resided in it. Their bleak, colorless forms created a swirling, opaque cloud on the otherwise dusty, maroon ground. After a brief moment of rolling her eyes in the direction of the soul-cloud, she inhaled deeply—flaring her nostrils as she confidently raised her arms towards the horizon.

A thunderous rumble emerged from where she was facing, and with a crash, a dense piece of black slate emerged and moved through the hole that was punched in the Void of Impossible Things. The slate disappeared out of sight as it fixed itself to the end of the bridge that extended far towards the Pre-Life. At the same time, in the deep, vastness of space, in a far remote corner of the Universe, an entire galactic system was crushed into absolute blackness. Every star and planet was snuffed out of existence, collapsing into massive black holes that cast out nothing but the Darkness coming from Helena. Through these holes, all forms of matter were swallowed whole, cascading their immense forms into dust and particles that slithered through to the After-Life, where every piece gravitated once more into massive sheets of dark grey slabs of rock, interlocking themselves like jigsaw puzzle pieces and assembling themselves onto the edge of the massive bridge. From the skies above the After-Life, another slate emerged, accompanied by another colossal clap of violent thunder.

Then another one appeared. Followed by another. Helena snapped the middle fingers of both of her hands and walked away. As she left the overlook, the boulders continued to appear. She made her way down the ever-spiraling stairs, listening to the cacophony of the echoing quake of her bridge being built. As she made her way to the grand, black-marbled throne room, she paused at the foot of her own throne to admire all that she had created. She soaked in her pride, bathed in her hubris as she flared her nostrils again with another large inhale. With that very breath, her hair shed itself of all of its remaining auburn color. As she ran her fingers through her once bushy mane, it became long stands of stringy, black hair. She snapped her fingers again, cascading a blackness all throughout her skin, like veins, as she descended the final steps that led to the front of the spire. She exited and sashayed across an enormous external pavilion that was soul-free, leading her right up to the foot of the black bridge; and there she stood, on the precipice of the bridge, as the sound of a pop rang out from behind her. The crashing echoes stopped as the bridge finished, and Elias appeared, carrying his oar in one hand and holding a chain in the other. The other end of the chain was fastened to a shackle that was secured to Father's neck. He hung his head limp and defeated in silence.

"I've arranged for some company to come along," Helena's words sliced through the thick air of silence.

Hesitantly, Elias spoke up. "Who's joining us?" he asked nervously.

"Not a 'who,' brother. More of a 'what.'" She teased and smirked as she began her long march across the floating, black walkway before the three of them. As soon as all of them began moving, large, ground-shaking footsteps began to follow them. Eli took a quick look behind him and saw three monstrous beasts following them: a three-headed hound that dwarfed Father even when he was at his biggest, a Minotaur-looking creature with enormous hooves and horns to match, and a flying squid-looking monstrosity with twenty-foot long tentacles that writhed aggressively as it pushed forward with the pack. After them, swaths of thousands and thousands of colorless souls condensed as they filled the bridge from wall to wall in back of everyone else.

Helena stopped abruptly and motioned behind without looking for her brother to give her the oar and he did so willingly, quietly relinquishing it to her, reluctantly parting with it once more. Helena took the oar and spun it upside down, placing the handle on the black rock beneath her. With a quick, firm tap on the ground, the oar transformed into a scythe, and the blackness from her hands spread like an infection into the weapon as the paddle bent and sharpened into a wicked prong. She tightened her grip on it, and with one hand, hoisted it as high as she could into the air. The skies above rapidly turned grey, growing darker and darker, cascading the After-Life into a fearsome pit, absent of light. In unison, Eli and Father, with the ancient beasts in suit and an armada of souls, followed the advance of their leader.

The bridge curved gently upward, higher and higher into the churning, blackened sky, as it stretched out for an immeasurable expanse. The skies above them lost their illustrious colors as the Realm dimmed to an ominous shadow with each of their silent, wordless steps.

• • •

Mother stood barefooted in the meadow facing the torn veil of the Void of Impossible Things with her back turned away from the Tree of Knowledge. The River Styx had begun to babble uproariously. In her chest, she could feel the wound in the fabric of the reality that she had created as she witnessed the rapid assembly of the ominously black structure that was barreling towards her and the entourage of anxiously fluttering souls that cowered and shook at her heels.

She looked down wishfully at the pile of clouds at her feet, and for a moment, the solemn look on her face dissolved into a visage of restfulness. "Be brave my children. Our moment looms." She heaved a heavy sigh and brushed a strand of her white hair away from her eyes before clapping both hands together twice.

The gargantuan branches of the Tree of Knowledge began to rustle from behind her, and after a brief moment, a trio of elegant, majestic-looking creatures emerged from the leaves and landed behind her confidently. A unicorn pranced around her in a small circle. It stood just as tall as her, if not taller when the incredibly long, dense, twisted horn perched atop its head was raised high into the air. An equally large Pegasus hovered above the ground to the left of her, and another to the right—both of their heavy bodies kept aloft by aggressive beats of their silver-feathered wings. They stood in front of the bell curve of the River Styx as it churned violently with the extra energy Helena was bringing into the Realm like a sea in a storm surge.

What was once nothing but a speck on the gloriously beautiful horizon of the Pre-Life, the black bridge was now something much more of an eyesore, bringing with it a grey haze of Darkness, destruction, and creation so bastardized that the fate of existence was now of consequence. Knowing the cost from the Universe of each of these bricks brought a single tear to Mother's wrinkled eyes as she realized that the last slates that Helena needed to finish her construction had just been brought into existence. A while longer, and Mother would see Helena and her siblings in tow as they approached from the descent of the arc, the massive silhouettes of the Ancient Ones ominously accentuated the skyline.

The River Styx crashed with a violent wave against the shore, sending the ferry—capsized and empty—clattering onto the meadowland. The sight of the empty boat was something she had not seen since the last Iteration. The absence of her children brought about a new wave of emotions—worry, concern, and foreboding. But she took another deep breath and began a slow march forward as the final piece of slate fell into place, finally completing the construction of the bridge. As she began moving, the cluster of souls stayed close to her feet, huddled for protection, and the three creatures each followed with a sense of dignity and readiness.

. . .

Her footsteps created a loud knocking sound as the heels of the boots that Helena wore clicked against the dense rocky bridge as she began her descending approach towards the Pre-Life. She gestured with one hand over her shoulder to her brother to stay where he was as she continued advancing, swaying her hips with a cocky swagger as she met Mother on approach. The two of them stared at each other, eyes locked in a grimacing salutatory stalemate, standing close enough that they could feel the other's breath on their skin. Helena's looked darker but younger than Mother had remembered, and inversely, Mother's skin had lightened and aged without grace. Helena's presence had brought with her a calamity the Pre-Life had never seen before—winds whipped through the meadow, tearing grass and flora up by the roots, massive surges of waves crashed through the River Styx, and the fabric of the Void of Impossible Things seemed to flail with the storm's strength.

"Helena," Mother greeted her daughter with stoicism.

"Mother," Helena returned as cordially as she could. "I trust you know why I am here." She twirled the scythe in her hands, the blade arcing like a lethal pendulum.

"You need my Essence—you want my power. You—You've recklessly destroyed that which has existed longer than you and held so much potential just so you could advance the Darkness to facilitate your own wicked machinations."

"Wicked machinations. Hah." Helena scoffed at Mother, pulling her face away and rolling her eyes with disgust. "Like you didn't plot against me, either, Mother. I know about your Vessel. I know about Madrina's little project away from the Pre-Life. I know you've asked Eliza to monitor and observe Eli and the rest of the siblings. Don't act superior, Mother, just because you did nothing. That's just like you, though—do nothing and hide in place."

"You think I did nothing, do you? Aside from Father and the twins, I may as well have been the only one doing my designated job and maintaining the Balance. For every soul that comes, another must go, and I have so diligently done that since before your genesis. Without the cycle of the After-Life and the Pre-Life, everything would come falling down. It would all be over before one of you children would even know what to do—Essence or no Essence."

"Speaking of which, Mother dearest, why are you holding out on me? Where *is* your Essence? I can't catch a scent of it in the slightest. What happened to you, you poor old hag?"

"Like I told you, dearest daughter," Mother mocked back to her child, "I have been working—doing what I am supposed to do. You and your siblings have always had a tendency of doing your own mischievous things, so this time, I elected to buy into it. At least a little bit. You see, what is it that I could do to ultimately stop your little rebellion, Helena? I could have had you banished. That's worked well for us, at least historically speaking, but Father would not have allowed it for even a moment. He's too fond of all of you after the last Iteration. So I had the children play—so to speak. While I was busy with the souls, I conducted the three of them like a symphony. They never missed a beat, and never failed to pull through, even when you and yours tried to interfere, we still stayed one step ahead of you."

Helena laughed uproariously at Mother's claim. "If that were the case, then where are they? Where are my little sisters and brothers? Where is my Essence?"

"It was never yours, and it will never be yours, Helena. You'd be wise to accept and understand that as best as you can before you either hurt or disappoint yourself."

"Well, I've come all this way, and I have to say, I am a bit disappointed." Helena sneered, casting a look of disapproval her way. "I thought there would be at least a little bit more of a welcome party than what I have received so far. A horse, some oversized birds, and a small handful of pitiful little souls? How pathetic. I guess it's time for you to die alone, like I always knew you would."

As if on cue, the rest of the Family came tumbling out of Eliza's magenta bubble and into the chaotic storm blowing around them. As quickly as she could, Eliza helped her siblings to stand up on their feet. She stood in front of them, wielding her oar defensively as she slowly backed up to distance them from the Hunter, who lay on the ground nearly motionless. Madrina and Davias braced each other in the confusion and calamity, processing the situation and preparing for the inevitable. Summoned by Helena, the Hunter slowly rose to his feet and hesitated for longer than a moment before staggering over to where Mother and Helena were staring each other down. He shot Mother an aggressive look as he walked past her and took his place beside his sister.

"Well, well," Helena sang, turning to face the late arrivals. "Our Family is finally reunited for the first time since the Iteration. Now let's get down to business."

CHAPTER 14

THE CHILDREN

Eliza was the first of the four siblings to gather her senses and survey the surroundings after emerging in the Pre-Life. She helped the other two to their feet as she locked eyes with a forlorn-looking Eli, who bore Father's restraints in his hands. Before them, the Hunter's body was crumpled in the dirt. Eliza picked up her oar and exchanged a worrisome look with her twin who looked past her. She followed his gaze and noticed the capsized ferry by the shore. A gust ripped through the meadow, and the darkened skies began to churn with a violent upheaval of wind and cold. Eliza retreated to be closer to Mother, holding the oar out defensively as she stared longingly towards Eli and stood in front of her other siblings.

After clamoring to his feet, the Hunter was frozen in place, uncertain of which move to make. In his mind, he knew he could strike either Madrina or Davias here and now, or he could take his place beside his sister in hopes he would be rewarded and not reprimanded. Before he could make the decision for himself, Helena barked to him over the roaring weather. "Hunter, you crow. By my side, now! Tell me what has come from your errand." He stammered a little as he trudged his way up to his sister's side, exchanging an equally passive-aggressive glance with Mother along the way. In his silence, Helena turned to the rest of the Family. "Well, well. Our Family is finally reunited for the first time since the Iteration. Now let's get down to business." She turned back to the Hunter expectedly.

Struggling to find the appropriate words to convey his failure, the Hunter began stumbling over his tongue as he approached Helena and her intimidating grip on her long-crooked scythe. "I'm sorry—I didn't . . .I couldn't. They were there before me. They got in the way." Her eyes followed him the entire time he was walking.

"Excuses!" staring directly at him, she shouted loud enough for the entire Family to hear. The creatures stirred at the sound of her voice. "I do not want to hear your excuses! I gave you a gift, and you squandered it, you pathetic bird-brain."

"I'm sorry, Helena. There was another child. I killed him, ripped his soul right out of his lungs. Had I known—"

"Silence, imbecile! I guess I'll have to change some plans now, since you have proven your incompetence. You can keep the gift I gave you, however . . ." She stepped closer to her brother, hoisted the scythe behind her, and without any hesitation swung and plunged the blade through the Hunter's chest. Every Family member gasped in unison as his limbs immediately went limp, and his eyes bulged in surprise. Helena lifted the blade up by the handle, dangling his body above her. Black blood poured out of the wound and down the scythe as it coated Helena's hands. Not a single sibling stepped forward in his aid.

After a moment, a black strand began to pull itself out of his body through the wound—like living flesh, the object, as opaque as night and dripping in dark blood, squirmed as it began to descend down the length of the handle until Helena grabbed it with one hand and began absorbing it through her skin, as if it belonged to her. It took seconds for her to finish, and when she was done, she put both hands back on the handle of the scythe and flung the Hunter's lifeless body far to the side of the meadow where he impacted with a crumpling sound and slid violently until his black blood began to soak and stain the ground. Helena spun around on the spot where she stood with her eyes closed. A cloud of black smoke and ash twirled around her like a cyclone. When she opened her eyes, she revealed two bowls of depthless, inky pits and cackled malevolently. All of the Ancient creatures on both sides continued to stir and grow restless. Helena turned her head to stare at the Hunter's mangled body—his limbs were twisted, and his concaved chest slowly rose and fell with each of his sputtering breaths. With her eyes turned away from them, Davias turned to Madrina, and the two of them nodded to each other in silent understanding.

"At long last he finally proved to be of some use," Helena spat with a disgusted grimace. "I was tired of him getting in the way."

Eliza choked down a large lump in her throat and cried out, "Helena! What did you do to him?" As she tried to step forward, Mother quickly reached out a single arm and wrapped it defensively around her daughter. Helena's attention turned to the two of them. She snickered as she watched Eliza struggle against Mother's hold.

"I want that oar," Helena hissed towards the two of them. While she was distracted, Madrina and Davias seized their opportunity to rush to the Hunter's place on the side of the meadow to check on his wounds. Madrina used both of her hands to roll him off of his back and onto his side. Her hands got covered in his thick, tarry blood in the process. Davias swept strands of hair out of his face, trying to find any signs of consciousness. They both nervously glanced back at their sisters, too distant to hear what they were saying. Eliza continued to struggle against Mother's hold, and Helena seemed to inch ever closer to the two of them.

"What are we going to do, Madrina?" Davias asked in a hushed whisper.

She ignored his question, "I can see him breathing; I can feel his chest. Is he even still in there?"

"Yeah, I can feel him in there," Davias said casually, as if the nonchalance of sensing his brother's consciousness was nothing new to him.

"What do you mean, Davias?" his sister asked him in a hurried whisper. "How can you feel his presence?"

"I don't know how to explain it—I can feel anyone in our Family. Each of you lights up my senses differently. I feel warmth around Mother, around you there's a cool mist and the smell of the meadow's dew. Ever since he hurt me, I taste blood whenever he's near. He's in there—I taste it."

Madrina looked at her brother as if he had been keeping secrets from her. She quickly finished processing what he had said and responded. "What should we do? Should we leave him here?"

"Use Mother's Essence, heal him enough so that he'll survive this ordeal. We'll move him closer to the River and out of harm's way," he suggested.

Madrina argued. "I'm not healing him—he doesn't deserve it. Everything he has done has been to spite us at every point along the way."

"Madrina," Davias raised his voice to a loud whisper. "Everything he has done has been at the command of Helena. We were complacent, too. Do not fault him for being as obedient as we were in this war." Davias then grasped his sister's wrists and placed them directly upon the Hunter's wound. He scrunched his face in intense focus, and Madrina's hands began to glow. The torn shreds of flesh and skin began fusing back together underneath the lake of blood that had collected on his chest.

Madrina gasped, "How are you doing this?" as she watched her brother heal the Hunter with her own powers. Unsure of how he was managing what he was doing, Davias found himself stammering for any words that might make sense because he himself truly didn't know. Before he could make a noise, their attention was captured by the sounds of screaming erupting from behind the two of them.

By the time they had turned to look, Eliza had managed to escape from Mother's grasp with the oar in her hands wielded like a weapon. Mother had screamed after Eliza as she charged at her sister, poised to attack her. Helena parried her advance with her scythe, and in the same fluid motion, continued spinning her blade towards Eliza. The curve of the metal caught the side of her arm, tearing a clean gash down half of her skin. Eliza managed to hold on to the oar but released her grip on it with her wounded arm. She took off running towards Davias and Madrina. As she gathered speed and approached the two of them, she struck the oar into the ground and vaulted herself with increased speed into the air.

Then, she vanished in a purple bubble high above them. The oar was sent flying and landed paces away from the two of them. Davias and Madrina quickly scanned the area for any sign of her, fearing the worst. Madrina made a quick scramble to recover the discarded oar.

After a split second, she re-emerged, higher up in the air with an increased velocity. Using her body as a projectile, she bulleted straight towards Helena, connecting with a direct hit square in her chest. Helena—caught completely off guard—dropped the scythe as she was hurled backwards onto her bridge. The creatures behind her growled and roared in her defense as they rose into protective stances. Eliza picked up the scythe and wielded it with confidence, ready to face Helena as she returned to her feet. Straight ahead of her, she saw the cloud of colorless souls stir aggressively, waiting for their command. She chanced a peek at Eli, who tightened his grip on Father's chains out of fear.

As Helena rose to her feet, she balled her hands into tight, dense fights that began to drip black tar onto the surface of the bridge as she advanced. She motioned with one of her hands to quell the commotion behind her as she lunged quickly with her long legs, flailing her fists wildly like ribbons. Eliza countered each desperate attempt to strike her with ease as the black liquid from Helena's hands spattered the area with dark spots. Madrina and Davias worked quietly to move their incapacitated brother closer to the River. When they had finished dragging his body to the bank, they regrouped with Mother as she shielded them from harm. Madrina clutched the oar as tight as she could to her side.

Meanwhile, Helena began using her longer legs to her advantage over her sister and started advancing with kicks and more aggressive lunges. When she couldn't keep up with her sister's advances, Eliza began teleporting out of the way, using her own lunges to gather speed and momentum between jumps leaving magenta streaks behind her. Pretty soon, the meadowland in front of the bridge was obscured with black and purple blurs of rapid movement, and every conscious Family member had their attention drawn to the scene. Eli and Mother were both holding their breath. The melee continued for several minutes until all motion came to a sudden halt. The blade from Eliza's scythe was buried in Helena's gut, and a steady outpouring of black ooze began to spurt from Helena's chest. There was a cheer from Mother and Eli as they watched. Helena coughed and spit up a thick stream of her blood as she stared her sister straight in the eyes. Helena pulled back one of her fists and quickly jabbed it into Eliza's chest, rupturing her breast and ribs. The hole created by her fist had caused Eliza to jolt, relinquishing her hold on the scythe. Still captured by the hand inside of her ribcage, Eliza tried to escape, but when she tried to teleport, the usual magenta bubble had turned coal-black and wobbled weakly, before popping without any effect. Eliza's body began to slump as

Helena wrenched the blade from her sternum with her free hand, shucking it onto the ground before her; her hand that was inside of Eliza's body began to search for her soul—her Essence. Eli began to scream from behind the two of them, and Helena shot him a lethal warning stare to silence him and his protests.

It didn't take long, and once she had found what she was looking for, Helena's fingers began to absorb the Darkness, the Life, and everything else inside of Eliza. Again, Eliza tried her best to teleport away from her sister, but the bubble this time appeared even weaker and shattered into nothing. As he watched from his place, Eli collapsed to his knees in muted desperation, still grasping onto Father's chains tightly.

Eliza's body went completely limp as her skin began to disintegrate. Her hair, her clothes, every piece of her began to dissolve into a purple dust that scattered unceremoniously in the wind. Eli, still on his knees, stifled a loud whimper. Madrina and Davias had just regrouped with Mother who held them tightly as the three of them looked on. Mother began to sob quietly, and Father didn't seem to react at all. Not a word came from the seven of them. Helena held her stomach with one hand as she picked up the scythe from the ground.

She used the scythe to brace herself upright. "Two down, four to go. Eli, bring Father forward," she commanded through heaving gasps.

"NOOO! Eli, don't do it!" Mother cried out. "Stop this, Helena! You've done enough!" Mother watched helplessly as Eli began to ascend to his feet—his face stricken with glistening tears.

Helena cast a wicked, black finger towards her creator and waved it wildly as she bellowed. "No, Mother. I don't think I have. I think it's you who has done enough. You and Father here need to answer for what you have done. To me, to us—your children. Wasting Iterations. Wasting creation. *EVERYTHING!*" She cried out with malice. "It's so funny that you try to uphold the Balance so badly when your contributions, in actuality, will surmount to its upheaval. Now you will come forward, and you will watch. Then, you too will die. Now, Mother. Eli, I won't ask again. Give these two a chance to say goodbye before I take everything from them."

Helena walked away from her spot and retreated into the swath of souls that embraced her like a protective mob. She stared out over them as she watched Eli march Father forward, guiding him with his shaking hands. With each of his tremors, the chains shook violently, casting an ominous rattle through the otherwise silent scenery. When Eli and Father passed Helena, she narrowed her eyes and followed the two of them with a confident grin and an amused chuckle. She placed her hand on one of Father's hunched shoulders and limped her way forward, leaning on him and her scythe for balance. The extra weight that Father had to bear caused him to stumble and fall to the ground where Helena kicked him, demanding him to stand back up.

"On your feet, you old fool! Mother, would you like to join him? Say any final words that might still be lingering on your mind?"

"Be wise, Mother!" Davias warned with whispered words from his position beside her. "Helena aims to kill the both of you."

"I'm well aware of that, my son. This has long been her endgame, and she proceeds ever closer to her goals. Madrina, protect that oar at all costs. Use it if you have to. Remember to use the Vessel if things start to seem . . ." she paused, choosing her next word carefully. "Desperate. At this point, it's not about maintaining the Balance or fulfilling your duties anymore. Helena has created too much of a disturbance for that now. For you two, it is about surviving at all costs."

"What about you, Mother?" Madrina pleaded, pulling on the hem of Mother's sleeve with the hand not clutching the oar.

"For me, now it is all about my ending. Children, I hope you know I will not make it out of these next moments alive, so I must serve my final moments with grace. Your sister now wields the power of the Hunter, along with the Essence of Darkness—she wasn't just about to kill Eliza, she absorbed her energy, and she will use that to eliminate both me and Father together. So she was right; I must answer for everything I have done. The lies, the obfuscation. The plotting, scheming, running around in secrecy. My atonement begins here. Now." She pushed Madrina's hand off of her robe and turned back to look at her one last time. "If you would please, protect each other. You both know what to do." Mother gave Davias one last look as well before she broke free from her place. The creatures behind her bowed their heads mournfully, and the thousands of colorful souls that looked on began to sway from side to side in unison.

Mother approached Helena and Father with tangible apprehension. Her eyes were fixated upon the top of Father's head as his gaze was cast downward. Without his Essence, every inch of his body had begun to reveal how archaic he actually was. His hair was thinning and withered. His skin was ashen and wrinkled. His shoulders were hunched, and his limbs hung weakly in submission. She reached out with one of her long, elegant arms and caressed his chin with just a stroke from her index finger. He brought his chin upward to meet Mother's gaze—dreary and empty, his eyes had lost all color.

"So," from behind a forced smile she whispered to him, "after all we have been through. The running, the hiding—all of creation has brought us to this moment."

Father blinked slowly, trying to hide the guilt behind his eyelids. "Yes," was all his deep, breathy voice could croak.

"Can you still feel it? The hum of the Universe and everything we have created?" Father shook his head remorsefully, closing his eyes so he wouldn't have to show the sadness he felt. Mother's smile widened. "I can," she said. "It's more beautiful now than it has ever been before. I can hear melodies of the past and songs of the future. Caged souls singing songs of freedom. The laments from the lost, looking for home and the jubilations of those who are loved."

"Why are you telling me this?" Father rasped.

"To give hope to the hopeless. This is not the end, Father. We both know what Helena will do. Eliza may be gone, but you need to remember that we have five other children that will manage. We will continue to exist in the Void—it is from us it was created, so it is there that we will rest for eternity. But we can watch, and we can listen. You will hear the song of the Universe again. Will you listen to it with me?" Mother cradled his cheek with the palm of her outstretched hand, and Father gently closed his eyes in response.

"We've made mistakes," his low voice grumbled. Then he corrected himself, speaking a little louder. "*I have* made mistakes. I was made to be arrogant, and I bought into it gladly, drunken with power. Be glad you were never inundated with the Darkness, Mother. It can confuse and disorient—perverting and twisting the wielder. I was a fool to weaponize it. I was a fool to let it drive us apart. I've had time to reflect on my existence now that I am free from the shackles of the Darkness. I am now afraid to admit that I was wrong." He continued speaking louder. "I am afraid because I know all the secrets that the Darkness has to offer. I am terrified of what *she* will do with it when she learns. I want to know what secrets Life has to offer, dear—I never got to experience it. I felt it briefly—each time we Reiterated I felt the fire and the light that you feel. The Darkness, it's very cold. I always wanted to feel more Life."

"All this time, Father, and you never said a word. Is that the reason for all of our fighting, the ruination, the eons of deception?"

Remorsefully, with his eyes still closed, Father managed an airy response. "Yes," was again all he said. Mother closed her eyes.

Though Madrina had inherited her Essence, she still held on to one fragment of Life inside of her for just this moment—a shard of warmth, sheltered within her lungs. It began to unravel, sending strands of energy to her limbs. The energy coursed through her outstretched arm until tiny filaments of light arced from her hand to Father's skin. His face lit up with a glowing smile as he felt it—Life—pulsing in his body. He exhaled peacefully. "I understand now. The meaning of Life. Thank you, Mother." He opened his eyes to see her smiling down towards him. Behind him, Helena replaced her hand on his shoulder as she sapped away what little energy Mother had imbued him with. She grew impatient, and with her new energy, she stood upright once again.

"That's enough!" She bellowed and hauled Father to his feet by the chains and shackles that bound him. "I grow tired of meaningless dialogue. It's time for some real change!" She released the chains from her grasp and wielded the scythe in both of her hands. She pulled the blade back and snarled viciously before bringing it down in a grand motion, effortlessly splitting Father in two, diagonally down his torso. Mother immediately clasped her hands to her mouth as both halves of his body fell to the ground with a slight thump. Black smoke rose from both parts until the body dissipated into nothing. Mother stood there shocked and speechless.

"Helena, you must stop!" Davias demanded. His sister began to laugh again. She wielded the scythe in front of her, pointing the handle menacingly towards her brother.

Her laughter ceased abruptly, and she responded with mockery. "Or what, Davias? You're going to try and stop me? My little sister and brother with their reassembled oar and half an army of souls. Do you think your Ancients can take on mine? Mine are much bigger and stronger than yours, and now Mother has no energy left. So she's next!"

Without any warning, Helena took the scythe and swung

the blade recklessly into Mother's sternum with full force. The curved hook of the blade stuck straight out of her back. Mother's Ancient creatures roared to life, wings flapping and hooves flailing in the air. Slowly, like blood flowing from a wound, a blissful white light began to emerge from both tears in Mother's torso. Weakly, she took her shaking hands and placed them on the handle. Helena's grasp was stronger, and before Mother could attempt to do anything, she yanked her weapon back out. Mother slumped to her knees as the light from her chest grew stronger and brighter until it was absolutely blinding. The illumination grew, lighting up the sky until a soundless burst sent out a supernova of light and energy, casting a violently strong gust of wind. Helena was swept off of her feet and thrown backwards, disappearing into her mob of souls. Every single sibling shielded their eyes and braced themselves from the fallout. When the winds had settled and the light faded down, each of the children slowly unshielded their eyes one by one. In turn, they all saw the creatures poised offensively and unmoving, facing off against the opposition. The sky was churning, turning darker, and a strong wind remained.

Madrina quickly turned to Davias, and in the same moment, she spun the oar with a flourish in her hands. Quicker and quicker it spun, releasing a soft humming melody until it shimmered. The wood hardened into a crystalline blade with a metallic-blue hilt. It sung as it moved through the air. "Davias," she said urgently, "you and the Hunter need to get out of here. It's time for you two to Vessel. Get to the water; you know what to do."

Davias reached out an arm and clutched his sister's shoulder, "What about Eli?" The two of them looked over to their youngest brother who had not moved from his spot. His eyes were still locked on the place where Eliza had perished.

"What about him?" Madrina dismissed, replacing her eyes back on their threatening sister. Helena was still reorienting herself.

She hadn't even made it out of the colorless cloud behind her.

"We need to save him, too. She'll kill him, Madrina. He's still our brother," he pleaded with her.

"If you can get through to him, then save him. Otherwise, he's a lost cause. Mother wanted us to save ourselves."

Offended, Davias stood his ground. "No, you're wrong! Mother wanted to save the *Family*, Madrina. So that's what I am going to do. You go fight our sister; give her everything and then some." In a gesture of love and departure, he squeezed her shoulder tightly, before dashing away towards the Hunter's lifeless body at a full sprint. "Eli, I need you! Eli!" he shouted along the way. He chanced a look over his shoulder and noticed his younger brother's attention had finally turned towards him.

Behind him, Madrina stepped forward and placed herself at the ready with her crystal-blue sword out in front of her. Behind her, the colored souls had mobilized. A small group had moved themselves to stand defensively in front of her, with larger groups flanking her sides. The three equine creatures at her side paced back and forth impatiently, while staring down their more monstrous brethren. Helena pushed her way forward through her army. Her souls remained unorganized and conglomerated behind her. Madrina's body arced with blue electricity as she waited for Helena to reach her mark just a few feet in front of her. The wind whipped at the scenery. The branches of the Tree of Knowledge groaned and bent with the force of the gusts. The two sisters' hair bellowed behind them; Helena's black, bushy hair tangled into a thick mane, and Madrina's smooth, white strands floated like a cape.

Davias continued scurrying to the Hunter. He was struggling against the strong winds until he felt a familiar weightlessness as a lavender bubble closed around him, and he and Eli appeared together at the edge of the River Styx, standing over their unconscious older brother. "Help me toss him in the water, Eli,"

Davias panted, wasting no time. He picked his brother up by the shoulders. Eli didn't budge from his landing spot, nor did he make a sound. He looked Davias in the eye, but made no reaction to what he was saying. "Eli, help me. Please. We need to go." A gut-wrenching roar ripped from the mouth of the bridge behind them, startling them both. Eli jumped to life and grabbed the Hunter's legs. In unison, they looked at each other and nodded one time before swinging and releasing his body into the water, which simply passed through the surface without making a splash.

"You next, Eli. You touched the Vessel; you can make it," Davias urged his sibling before watching him hesitate, then jump off and plunge straight through the water. Stealing one last look over his shoulder to check on Madrina, Davias followed suit and dove headfirst off the river bank.

CHAPTER 15

THE BATTLE

Darkness and Life surged from the wound pierced in the Void of Impossible Things by the black bridge. The storm-touched air crackled with a mixture of their energies. Alone together, Helena, the sister of Darkness, and Madrina, the sister of Life, stared at each other unblinking, unmoving; both waiting for the other to falter first. The respective audiences of souls visibly vibrated with an eager anticipation for what was to come. For their time to fight. To defend. A chance to be reborn again in a Universe all the same, or entirely different. The hurricane winds intensified, slicing through the meadow with aggressive speeds. Each of the six massive creatures poised for battle braced themselves against the gale.

Like a thunderclap, the mixture of Darkness and Life swirled in the atmosphere and boomed with an exploding burst. As if signaled by this, the gargantuan, three-headed hound—Cerberus—howled from each of its mouths with assertion, creating a chaotic symphony with the wind as it stepped forward. It lowered its front half and bared all three sets of teeth. It lashed out towards the closest Pegasus with an echoing bark from one of the muzzles as another attempted to gnash at one of the wings.

At the same time, the Kraken took off in flight with astonishing speed. Given its monumental size, it used its many appendages to hurl itself with effortless grace—spiraling through the air like a cyclone. On cue, the other Pegasus batted both wings against the winds and dove into a collision course that would intercept the opposition.

Motionless still, the sisters squared off in attempt to read the other. Beside Helena, her Minotaur towered over her, staring with his horned head and red eyes, stamping his cloven feet and whipping a pronged tail in his wake. Madrina was protected by the Unicorn who stood at her side, her broad, muscled hide pressed close to the sibling's body, staring forth and tense with anticipation. In unison, both creatures took off at full speed, charging at the other with heads lowered and horns outstretched. The sound of galloping mixed with the rest of the violent cacophony. Midstride, the two collided. The Unicorn's horn pierced the abdomen of the Minotaur. Angry, the Minotaur picked the Unicorn up by her belly using his massive arms, pulling the protrusion back out of his body. With a huff and a flare from his nostrils, he flung the Unicorn back onto the ground, meters away from Madrina, who broke her petrified stance in order to guard herself. Her eyes shifted to the creature who landed beside her, and while she was momentarily distracted, the Minotaur took the open opportunity to begin rushing straight towards her. The Unicorn attempted to scramble back up in time. The Kraken had begun attempting to ward off its Pegasus defender by making punching motions with numerous tentacles. The nimble, winged creature was able to evade many of these shots, taking an occasional blow to its body, but it was unable to respond to the Minotaur's advance. Much like the other Pegasus, who found itself dodging multiple mouths snapping and snarling at its wings in an effort to bring it down to the ground.

Madrina sensed the situation. Her eyes shifted to the Minotaur whose current advance had him trampling a handful of paces away. With one quick flourish, Madrina crossed her feet and spun on the spot, tactfully swinging her blade across her midsection. From the crystal-blue material, she cast out a blasting wave of white-blue light that met the monstrosity square in the chest, pushing him back with ease. The Unicorn managed to bring itself back to its feet as Madrina swung the sword again, sending another blast that swept the red-eyed beast off of its feet, hurling it backwards.

Helena took her scythe and pounded the ground beneath her feet with it. A rippling wave of bubbling tar ripped through the terrain, snaking towards Madrina at a fearsome pace. Without a moment to spare, Madrina skirted the assault with a diving roll towards the Unicorn. The majestic creature bowed her knees briefly to allow Madrina to mount her, and then the two of them charged forward towards the staggered Minotaur. As they rushed, Madrina swung her blade yet again, this time aimed straight at her sister. If she wasn't moving, her attack might have hit its mark. Instead, the energy wave veered to Helena's right and the Minotaur hauled itself back onto its two feet. Behind it, the swarm of black and grey souls swelled like a wave and spilled forth like a thick, dark fog, rolling in quickly. The unified rainbow brigade of souls defending Madrina mobilized as well, clashing forth with their ill-commanded kin.

Above them, battles waged on between the two Pegasuses and their foes. The Kraken, still aloft, had managed to ensnare the stallion in a constricting tentacle. The Pegasus screamed out a bleating cry as it struggled against the grip. It writhed and twisted against the confinement until it was able to free one of its wings. With all of its might, the Pegasus beat that wing, scattering silver feathers in the slashing wind. Combined with the hurricane force and the extra gusts from the Pegasus, the Kraken's strength weakened enough that the captive was able to break free. With a full wingspan stretched out wide, the creature rode the current of the storm, gaining speed and momentum until it circled back around, landing in the center of the Kraken with a head-butt and a deafening smack.

The other Pegasus was having better luck with the Cerberus, using a similar tactic as the first. It was launching itself into the necks of the hound, using its muscular wings and hooves to deal bone-breaking blows. With each impact, the Cerberus released a pained, barking yelp from the depths of one of its jowls. It lashed out with a heavy paw, managing to scratch the underside of one of the rippling wings, sending the creature into a feather-raining free-fall. It managed to catch itself in mid-air just above the ground, but a moment later, the other front paw came crashing down, cratering into the land. It missed by a mere margin. The golden flora and fauna that decorated the land were sent scattered in a strong shockwave that provided assistance for the Pegasus—lifting it up into the air for its next flight. It continued circling and striking once again, prolonging the ebb and flow of the struggle.

Everything was happening around the two sisters, whose menacing stares at one another were disrupted only by Madrina's chest-heaving breaths as she dismounted her equine companion and Helena's under-the-breath laughter. Assertively, Helena took the handle end of her scythe and jammed it into the ground several times, sending wave after wave of rippling tar chasing after Madrina, who only had a spare moment to react. Casually, she swung her sword in front of her three times—creating an unseen wall that parted the waves of blackness. They splashed off to the sides, which narrowly missed the Unicorn but had landed a ricochet onto the Cerberus. The massive front-left paw of the hound immediately began to smoke—as if an invisible fire had been lit. Madrina charged through the parted tar, wielding her sword in front of her as her feet pounded deep footprints into the black and gold soil of the battleground. At the same time, the Unicorn rushed forward beside her. Using the broad body of the creature as a shield, Madrina swung out her sword again, to her side, casting her blue energy in the direction of the Cerberus as the Unicorn darted forth, skewering the Minotaur's torso once again.

The arc of energy exploded against the Cerberus, creating a massive white explosion. The Pegasus—who had still been circling through the air—was thrown backwards, creating a shower of silver feathers that scattered in the high winds. The hound was knocked clear off of its feet; its left head had lost half of its face—leaving behind charred, black sinew. The remaining two heads howled loudly in pain. Madrina pivoted where she stood and sent another blast airborne towards the Kraken while the Unicorn reared its powerful neck muscles, lifting the Minotaur off its feet as it continued charging back towards the bridge.

The lightning that Madrina sent skyward also made direct contact. Stunned, the Kraken began to fall from the sky, cratering into the ground below. Empowered by the speed of the storm, the remaining airborne Pegasus dove headfirst into the crater. Thick pieces of rubble and stone were sent flying as the shockwave rang out like a bell's toll.

Madrina turned again, facing her sister in time to see her approaching with speed. Helena's scythe swung ominously with each swift stride. As she leapt forward, Madrina readied her sword. Metal rang out as she countered Helena's first advance. Then her second and third. Helena bore down with her offense, making desperate, semi-calculated swings with her curved blade. Madrina, meanwhile, bided her patience—waiting for a clear opening in her sister's position while parrying each advance that she could manage. Their arms danced with their weapons as their partners, each of them in time with the other's motions and movements.

A terrible cracking sound reverberated over everything else, originating from the mouth of the bridge where the Minotaur and Unicorn were locked in a stalemate. The Minotaur had regained his footing, hooves dug into the soil, still pierced through and through by the single prong of his opposition. With a snap of its hips, the Minotaur split the Unicorn's long, twisted horn down the seam. He placed both muscular hands on the neck of the silver beast and pressed it down into the rocky surface of the bridge, then dropped the rest of his weight on top. The Unicorn released a bleating whine as a handful of the bones in her body snapped or shattered from the blow.

The wall of souls violently clashed in the tempest, creating blasts of colors as entities eradicated their existence in order to further the cause they were conscripted to. Helena slowly began to alter her footwork, dancing now in a wide circle around her sister, who made strides to keep the distance between the two while managing to avoid the craters, creatures, and other obstacles that the chaotic scene had to throw her way. The Tree of Knowledge groaned even louder against the weight of the strain. Helena was hyper-focused on her assault; while she swung and she slashed, Madrina learned the patterns of her movements. She would swing, then cross her feet and move slowly to either side as she pulled back and readied herself for another attack. Thinking she may have found her opening, Madrina bought herself a little more time.

The crater, now immediately in front of her and behind her sister, clamored with massive tentacles flailing from beneath the surface. The Kraken was trying to climb out of the hole its body had created, but the flying Pegasus above it was darting in the air, back and forth into the crater—pulverizing its own body with each collision. With no help from Madrina, mutually assured destruction was the only way it would overcome its foe, and so it continued to throw itself into the ground, harder and harder with each strike. Soaring higher and higher into the atmosphere, it rallied with one final loop in the sky before bolting into the ground with such tremendous speed that the silver feathers stuck to its wings began to glow and resonate with an aggressive hum. A blinding explosion of light obscured the scene. The resulting blast split the Kraken into several pieces, each of them leaking a thick black ooze into the once rich and radiant soil. The illuminating light lingered for mere moments before conceding to a massive frenzy amongst the dichotomized groups of souls.

In the middle of all of the chaos, the two-headed Cerberus and the remaining Pegasus were just regaining their footing. Part of the Pegasus's right wing was singed and missing half of the feathers. The Cerberus stood on three of its behemoth paws—the fourth one was still smoldering from the acidic tar that Helena had conjured. Having both been injured, their fight continued at a much slower pace on the surface. The Cerberus was reduced to snapping at the Pegasus with one or both of its remaining mouths, while the other beast shielded itself from the advances using its one good wing and nimbly hopped out of the way when it couldn't. Just like Madrina, this creature was buying its time, looking for an opening in its adversary's assault while the sisters were busy with their own melee.

Helena swung with her curved blade.

Madrina parried with her sword and riposted with her own attack.

Helena countered hastily, putting her back on the offense.

Violent sparks emerged from the clashing weapons. Their feet danced like everything had been choreographed beforehand.

And again, the cycle would repeat. Parry, riposte, countered with a shower of red and blue sparks. The wall of souls swelled and billowed, pressing in on the siblings, restricting more and more of their space.

A wailing cry ripped out of the Unicorn as the Minotaur grabbed on firmly to her braided horn. With as much might as it could muster, the monster snapped the spear off of the horse's head. The Unicorn began lashing about from side to side until it was stilled by the monstrous hands once more. With a firm grip on the creature's neck, the Minotaur began constricting, tighter and tighter until the Unicorn's lashing stopped and her body slumped to the soil. No horn and no signs of life. The Minotaur howled, releasing a spray of mist from its snarled snout as it charged off towards the Pegasus and the wounded hound.

The three of the remaining Ancient Souls met with catastrophic consequences. The Minotaur charged headlong into the Pegasus as it shielded itself from a snapping maw from the two-headed Cerberus. The horns punctured the body of the Pegasus, who released a similar scream to the Unicorn and writhed in excruciating pain as it was hoisted up in mid-air. The marred center-face of the Cerberus straightened up tall on its three good paws and opened its jaws wide. Without warning, it came forth, crunching down deep with every single one of its jagged teeth. In an instant, the head of the Pegasus was missing, and its body went deathly still. Both creatures of Darkness released ground-trembling roars of victory and began to make their charge towards the final battlefield—the hound was limping along the way to the soul-cloaked scene.

With a flourish of her left hand, Madrina sent a wave of her souls towards the on-comers. Unified, they catapulted forward with turbulent force like a striking cobra. The cloven Minotaur was able to evade with ease, but the Cerberus was met with a tremendous percussion as it was brought back to the ground by the train of souls who snaked their way into the air and recoiled straight through the back of the beast, burrowing in the belly.

The Cerberus stopped moving as it ballooned to a bulbous state, bursting open wide with an extravagant display of colors. Showers of black flesh, sinew, and innards littered the meadow like an eruption of oil scattered through the whipping winds.

Galloping on his two hooves, the Minotaur hurled forward, gaining speed and losing the distance between him and Madrina. As he grew dangerously near, a number of Madrina's remaining souls scooped her up and lifted her out of harm's way. From her ethereal platform, she struck out towards the Ancient beast and severed the horns cleanly from his head. She leapt from the air and led her descent with the blade angled outward. Effortlessly, she sliced through the center of the Minotaur, splitting it into two heavy halves that tumbled to the ground where he stood. Helena unleashed a wicked shriek, cocking her arms backwards and arching out the rest of her body. She was at a safer distance now. Madrina struck forth with her lightning.

Bracing herself, Helena was shielded from the blast with a wall of her own souls who perished instantly. Flash! Another blast erupted from Madrina's blade, and again, Helena sent more of her dwindling army to their demise, bursting into smoke and nothingness. Hair flowing behind her in the wind like a cape, Madrina continued siphoning off the rest of her energy with each swing of the blade. Clouds of condemned souls were vanquished one after the other until there were none left for Helena to hide behind. Madrina's sapphire eyes glowed brighter with electricity as she concentrated the last of her plentiful energy into one final bolt. In a reckless rush, Helena sent forth one massive tidal wave of bubbling Darkness—the tar that boiled up from the ground enveloped a large area and pressed forward as the lightning bolt struck the black scythe in Helena's hands. It shattered—splintering into millions of tiny shards. Madrina quickly took the blade and plunged it into the soil before her, creating a shockwave that knocked back the oncoming wave from her sister. The two forces collided with each other, cancelling one another out. The storm continued to rage around them. The meadow was destroyed. The water from the River Styx was surging up the banks. The branches from the Tree of Knowledge looked like they were about to break.

Both disarmed, they panted heavily and stared deep into the other's eyes. Helena's flashed with a crimson fury. Madrina's sparked with a bright, blissful blue. Helena began a slow, eventful advance. Nearby, Madrina spotted the severed horns that had fallen from the Minotaur's head. As Helena continued her slow shamble forward, Madrina made a quick move to grab both of the horns in each of her hands. Clutching them tight she sprinted and leapt forward with all of her strength. Her arms swung like pendulums as she came down and forward. Madrina plunged both of the horns into her older sister's chest. Black blood poured out of the open wounds. She staggered backwards and clutched the protrusions. She growled angrily and slumped forward onto her knees. She pulled the horns from her chest and more blood cascaded forth, staining the soil with wretched tragedy.

A raspy growl whispered from the elder sister's throat. "This. Isn't. Over."

Mercifully, Madrina stepped forward and placed her right hand on her sister's heaving shoulder. Helena batted her hand away scornfully.

"You. Can't. Kill. Me," she wheezed. "You can't even touch the Darkness, sister!" The storm around then began to quickly subside.

"You can have the Darkness all to yourself. You'll need it in order to run this place. Though, I know you won't. So, I'll be back, and we will settle things then."

"You can't leave; your Vessel left without you," Helena taunted.

"Who said there was ever only one? I've had a backup this entire time. It was my own Vessel, and now you won't be able to find me. Without a Watcher by your side, you can't leave. You'll be just as imprisoned as us."

"I'll be waiting for you! When you return, I will annihilate you. I will use everything it takes to erase you and our worthless brothers from existence. Mark my words, *heathen*." She hissed her final word.

"Consider them marked," Madrina responded. "I expect you'll be waiting. We will, too." With those words, she took her hand back and began striding towards the edge of the River and without hesitating, she dove in, straight through the surface, slicing through it like a blade and descending to the other side. To Life.

CHAPTER 16

THE MEANING OF LIFE

There was no color. No blackness. Only white. Endless white shapeless shifting shades. Nothing existed here, in the Void of Impossible Things. A vacuum of existence, a pocket outside of the Universe. The source of Time. It was wounded now and bleeding. A mixture of Life, Darkness, and Time cascaded into an abyss, like a waterfall placed at the end of everything.

There were no sounds. Through the white, all three of the brothers tumbled. Davias could sense both of the others drifting aimlessly through the ether. Anytime he thought he heard an echo of anything, it was muffled out—snuffed out into a muted whimper.

He could feel his energies reweaving inside of his body—like fabric repairing itself from its wear and tear. Life bound to Darkness, which bound to Life, both connected by Time intertwining. He felt cold and heated at the same time, like his bare nerves were being painted with gasoline.

The white was so blinding; he couldn't escape it even when he clasped his eyelids tight. He felt different here. Splintered, but at the same time complete. More knowledgeable now, like the Void had infused him with the tales it held. With his eyes closed, he could sense something—*someone*—reaching out.

"Mother?" he tried calling out with his voice, but the sound faded into absolutely nothing the moment he opened his lips. He waited while he floated, falling through the nothingness. "Eli?" He tried again but with the same, unproductive outcome. "Hunter?" This time, he asked with trepidation—but still no sound to be heard.

No response came. Just the endless sea of cosmic white.

Then it came again. Like a humming frequency, it was almost like he could feel it rather than hear it. "Davias."

"Mother?"

"Madrina." Disappointment pulsed through Davias.

Coming quickly to his senses, he asked, "Is everything okay? Are you hurt?"

"Unscathed," she said. "Helena's much worse for wear, but she'll survive."

Nervously, he followed up. "And the fallout?"

"The Ancient Souls are vanquished, as are millions of regular ones. Eli's oar was destroyed. Casualties of the cross fire. The Pre-Life will be scarred by the Darkness forever, and who knows what Helena will do with her powers in our absence.

"We can worry about that later. I'm using my own Vessel to escape. You need to recuperate your energy, and we need to strategize for whatever happens. Assume the worst from here on out, right?"

His soundless voice nervously replied. "You had a Vessel? Why? What does that mean? Where will I find you? Where will we end up?"

Madrina's disembodied voice bounced around in his head. "That depends on our Vessels. Where they are and where they go. We won't always have full control over that, yet. I can tell you that your Vessel will be drawn to mine like a beacon since I was the one that created him. Things will be different. For us and for them. It's important to remember that everything rides upon our Vessels now. It's worth quite a lot to know that we're mortal, until we are released from our Vessels."

"And that means—"

"Yes, Davias," his sister's voice cut off his train of speechless thought. "We'll have to terminate each other in order to get back. So, like I said, recuperate, strategize, and prepare." A thick silence followed her words.

"Madrina?" Davias finally reached back out.

"Yes?"

"How long do we have before . . ." his thoughts trailed off, unsure of how to phrase what was about to happen.

"I imagine you'll have to wait a while. Three of you in one body might take a little bit of extra energy. I, on the other hand, am almost ready."

Almost defiantly, he replied right away. "Are you ready, though?"

"I've been ready, little brother."

"I'll miss you. Until we reunite." Before he could finish his thought, Davias could feel the sudden absence of his sister. Abruptly burdened with the weight of loneliness, he descended through the white cascade endlessly and directionless. He closed his eyes, still able to see the light bleed through. Once his eyes were shut, he could faintly hear his younger brother, like he had suddenly tuned to a different frequency in his mind.

"Eli? Are you in here?"

Weakly the words came through. "Yeah. Do you know what happened to Hunter?"

"He's in here somewhere," Davias reassured. "I can feel him."

"I'll trust your judgement. Do you know where we are headed?"

"Is that a new feeling for you, Eli? Travelling through the Void but not knowing your destination," Davias tried mocking in a brotherly tone. "Sorry." He quickly apologized. "I don't actually know. Madrina told me it was up to our Vessels."

"You spoke to Madrina? That means the fight is over . . .What happened?"

"Helena still stands. She's isolated in the Realm. She said there was a lot of fallout from the battle. Lots of destruction. The Ancient Souls were killed. Eli," he paused before continuing. "Your oar was destroyed."

Without a breath in between, Eli replied, "What about Eliza's?" His cosmic voice sounded desperate, thickened with concern.

Davias admitted to his brother, "Madrina made no mention of the oar that we had. If it isn't destroyed, then it has to be up there somewhere."

"That's not good. We cannot afford for Helena to find that oar. The amount of power she has, she could make that the instrument of our destruction the moment we return." There was a lingering silence as the two of them nearly avoided the painfully obvious topic.

"Eli, I'm sorry about Eliz—"

"Don't you dare say her name! You. Mother. Madrina. *You* were supposed to protect her. You were supposed to *defend* her. She was *never* supposed to leave that damn ferry! She was never supposed to leave *my side*!"

Unable to sense the Hunter in the Void anymore, Davias tried to quell his sibling's angst. "Calm down, Eli. Nothing is your fault. Helena manipulated you—manipulated all of us. There wasn't a single one of us who wasn't under her heel at some point. What else could we have done?"

Desperation rang in Eli's thoughts as they waved through the Void. "I could have taken her to the most remote corner of creation and left her there. I could have dropped her in the Void and let her get ripped apart. We could have Vesselled her and locked *her* away!"

"And you don't think Helena wouldn't have used her powers to destroy half the Universe to escape whatever prison we concocted? At least this way, we're hidden. She can't find us. She can't destroy us. She can't even leave the Realm. The way I see it, Eli, this is the best-case scenario," Davias tried to reason with his sibling.

"Best-case scenario? My twin is dead! Eviscerated. Mother and Father are gone, and the Hunter is a lifeless sack of misery right now. Who knows where Madrina will end up. We're scattered, Davias. Like dust in the cosmos," Eli harrumphed pessimistically. "The only way we can all end up back together is either through tragedy or a miracle. Right now, I have a lot more stock in tragedies, so do me a favor and when we get to the Vessel, *leave me the hell alone.*"

Eli's final words reverberated like a threatening boom, leaving Davias alone to contemplate what might happen next as he watched the swirling atmosphere of white. If his brother was as angry at the Family as he was, he thought to himself, then being Vesselled with him was going to be anything but simple. He wondered how he might find Madrina, and where he might find himself. He began theorizing how it might feel to be mortal—to be bound to a Human.

He was suddenly interrupted. Another sense, another feeling invaded his mind. A sound, like a soft ringing in his ears—a whispered resonance that felt so familiar to him.

He closed his eyes, and he saw her face. "Mother!" he cried out with his soundless voice. He watched her smile. Her hand reached out as if to embrace a single one of his cheeks. Part of him thought he could feel her touch. "Mother," he said again more solemnly.

"My son," she sighed. "You made it out all right. How about everyone else?"

"Madrina's alive; she passed through the Void already—" he was abruptly cut off by Mother.

"I know," she said. He felt her fingers run along his chin. "I spoke to her before she Vesselled. She told me Helena still stands, millions of souls destroyed, and the last of the Ancient Ones were annihilated. How are your brothers?"

"I could feel the Hunter in here for a while. He wasn't conscious when we submerged him. I can't tell if he'll even wake up, and Eli—Eli is beyond upset. At you. At me, and Madrina. There's no reasoning with him. Mother, I don't want to be Vesselled." He could feel a tear roll down the curve of his cheek as he began to sob softly.

"Don't cry, my child," she calmed him and wiped away the tear with her celestially disembodied hand. "Know that at this point, you must be Vesselled. The reweaving process has already started."

"Will I see you again?" Davias pleaded through his soundless sobs.

"It's hard to say for certain, son. I'm scattered. I can only exist in the Void now, and with the Void bleeding, I can't see through. Helena controls the After-Life and the Pre-Life, so the only way you'll be able to access the Void is through your Vessel's dreams, but I may not be there. I may never be there again. Do you understand what I am saying? Once you pass through to Life, you may never see or hear me again."

The truth stung into his heart like a poison coursing through his veins. His breath was taken from his lungs. He began to feel the fibers of his body twisting and contorting—changing into something else. He could no longer feel below his ankles.

"Mother. Something's happening. I can feel my energy slipping."

"Then it has begun. You only have a few moments before you're completely rewoven into Life," she said with a sternness to her voice. "Anything I have to say to you has already been said.

You're my favorite child, Davias. If I could, I would undo every struggle that has led us to this point so we could exist in harmony. Life was my body, you know—not the energy, the planet. I created it out of my energy to shield and protect myself, so long ago. And now, my creation must protect you, my child."

"Mother?" he asked, choking through his sobs. The numb feeling in his legs had crept its way up to his knees. "I understand the Darkness, I think. It corrupts through creation."

"It corrupts through destruction. Creation with the Darkness must always come with a destructive price. That destruction will intoxicate with wicked power," she corrected him.

The feeling now was above his waist, and inching higher up his torso. "Then what is the meaning of Life?"

"The meaning of Life, Davias, has been and always will be family. Family and creation. We must create so that we can prevent the destruction of ourselves and our families—not just us, but everyone in Life. We leave behind legacies—stories to tell and moments to remember. Innocent creation. Lasting legacies. These are the things that give meaning to Life. Darkness will always be there. Waiting to destroy and corrupt. But Life exists to restore the peace and fill in the cracks of a painful eternity. Go, experience the creation that I have left for you. Do not miss me, for I live within you. Now and always. I love you, my child. You are the meaning of my Life."

Her voice faded into an incomprehensible muttering as he felt his chest disappear. Mother's hand slipped from his face. His nerves unwound from each other as his face began to dissolve, and the white from the Void of Impossible Things gave way to a brilliant, blue glow.

ABOUT THE AUTHOR

A fantasy writer born and raised in Scottsdale, Arizona, Mike Ekstrom creates tales that are bound to the mystic and ethereal while intertwined with the human condition. What began as a personal project going into college, *The Volumes from the Void,* has taken him over fifteen years to craft into a developing five-part series.

Having written since a young age, he has been able to combine his education of World Religions and his perspective as an Autistic individual to create unique characters, worlds, and stories based on the collision of musical inspiration and real-world scenarios. When he is not writing, Ekstrom finds his tranquility and escapism in a variety of mediums, whether those be video games, fencing, or the newest LEGO set.